Treasure Tales of the Shawangunks and Catskills

by HAROLD HARRIS

Published in Commemoration

of the Ellenville Sesquicentennial

1805 - 1955

The additional illustrations in this edition are from the Annual
Year books of the Holland Society and are over 100 years old.

DEDICATED TO

My wife Leslie
My children Wendy, David, and Kate
And my grandchildren Caleb and Maren

Table of Contents

6   Foreward
8   Preface
13   Introduction
18   Dutch Gold
25   Dutch Silver
30   Legend of Tongoras
32   A Story of the Ashokan
36   Legend of Unapois
39   Claudius Smith
43   Tory Treasure
45   Lost Silver Mine
47   Old 99
57   Variations on the Theme
61   Lost Gold Mine of the Hudson
66   Captain Kidd
72   Giants in the Earth
80   The Salt of the Earth
84   The Fountain of Youth
89   Hussey Hill Gold
93   There is Gold and Silver Too
101 The Blue Gold of the Catskills
111 Resorts
119 Epilogue
126 As Time Goes By
128 Alf Evers
130 The Ice Age
137 Bibliography

FOREWORD
by Alf Evers

Treasure Tales

Many writers have celebrated the alluring surface features of the Shawangunks and Catskill Mountains region, where mountain tops and waterfalls glitter in the sun, but Harold Harris has charmed us with a well-planned and well-written account of the brightest features of the world that lies beneath the surface mountains. He deals deftly with the tales told him by mountain people and the material that has found its way into print. He weaves it all into a series of very readable essays. Taken as a whole, it serves as a good history of treasure hunting in the region: the search for the silver of Dutch days, Captain Kidd's hidden loot, silver and gold buried for safety in the turmoil of revolutionary times. There is even the traditional tale of the bride-to-be who was buried only to be exhumed by would-be jewelry thieves. She frightened the grave robbers and rose again to lead a normal life.

A few years ago, a storm caused a slide on one of the southern Catskills. An old timer in the vicinity told me that when the slide happened, knowledgeable men from the surrounding country had hastened to the spot to look for signs of gold or silver because slides like this were God's way of revealing treasures He had buried in the sunless earth. When I asked if any treasure had been found at the slide, my informant said only, I dunno.

The old tales of treasure to be found -- if you go about it the right way in the Shawangunk Catskill region -- are still alive. They fascinated our grandparents, our children and our grandchildren. Mr. Harris fittingly concludes with accounts of the search in modern times for deposits of natural gas and oil in the region. So Treasure Tales live on among the people of our region.

Harold Harris has crafted with skill and spirit a book that is not only informative but also fun to read.

Preface

Writing this book was work, but gathering the material for it was fun. And in gathering this material, the pursuit of legends of treasure led me to many remote byways in the Catskills and the Shawangunks. As I closed in on my elusive legend I generally found myself sitting face to face with some old time resident of the mountains, and chatting about times gone by. After we had spoken for a while and the old timer realized that all I wanted was to talk about the old days, his reserve would thaw. Invariably, he would then turn the tables on me and the interview ran something like this.

"Are you from around here?" he would start.

"Well, I live in Ellenville, but originally I'm from New York City", I'd reply.

"How long are you up here?" would be his next question.

"Oh, about six years."

"Well, how in the world did you ever get interested in this sort of thing?" inevitably would come next.

Then it would be my turn to tell a story. It ran something like this. "I grew up in New York City and went to school there. Although I did some traveling, most of it at Uncle Sam's expense, I was a confirmed city dweller. Without complaint I breathed my quota of carbon monoxide and I could nimbly cross any street without regard for the traffic lights. I got seven hours of sleep nightly in my small apartment and one hour on the subway going to work in the morning. I knew none of my neighbors and less of the history of my city. And I was aware of the rest of the country by virtue of the fact that they sent baseball teams to play at our city's shrines, Ebbetts Field, Yankee Stadium, and the Polo Grounds.

This steel and concrete pattern was broken in 1948 when my work led me to where a new Television Antenna Plant was being started in Ellenville. I had never been there but had heard vaguely that it was a summer resort. I moved there with misgivings which were quickly dispelled and replaced by a feeling that I had never before experienced - a love for a part of our country. Never had such natural beauty been a part of my daily life.

The entire area and the people there filled me with a new curiosity. Most of my spare time was spent driving through the countryside and in time any unexplored road in the area became a challenge. When the primary and secondary roads gave out and the local towing service tired of pulling my car out of mud holes and ditches in abandoned roads, my explorations were continued through the acquisition of that latter day, "Tin Lizzie", the Jeep. During these expeditions, now accompanied by my wife (who also got the bug), we would see old ruins, unusual mountain forma- tions, or small communities, in unlikely places, with odd names. Later I would ask my acquaintances, many of them from old fami- lies in the area, questions about the things we had seen. To my surprise very few of the "natives" seemed to know anything about their wonderful country. Growing up in it, they took its splendor for granted and being modern they knew nothing of its history.

So in addition to exploring, I began to read about the area. In time, I had gone through all of the interesting old books (see bibliography) that I could beg, borrow, or buy and the exciting history unfolded for me. These activities still continue and I've become a confirmed explorer and collector.

At some point in the process, I began to feel that I'd like to make some contribution to the knowledge of the area for the enjoyment of those people for whom the Catskills and the Shawangunks hold special meaning. It would be foolish to attempt to write just another history. The saga of the early settlement of the Dutch over 300 years ago has been told many times. The old sources are all picked over and barring major finds, the history of the area is written.

In 1949 I came upon and explored the Old Spanish Tunnel in Ellenville. (See Page 85) This remarkable mine, the origins of which are completely unknown, fascinated me. What were they after? How many other such mines might there be? In my reading in different books, I noticed that there were stories or legends concerned with similar subjects and very few appeared in more than one of these obscure old books. I began collecting them from their old sources. Out of curiosity I tried tracking down the location of the mines. Then to my surprise, I found in speaking to the old timers, they would say, "No I never heard of that treasure but did you ever hear of - - - - - - - - - ?" and off I would be on another expedition. There were many such stories and incidents and so this work became the natural outgrowth of the curiosity. And, of course, that curiosity grew from grandeur of the Catskills and the Shawangunks."

One old timer who spent his declining years reading, heard the reply above. He said, "I understand how it is with you". He ~ot up from his rocker and took a book from a shelf. He thumbed through it and copied something out of it. He then said, "If you ever write that book and are called upon to explain why, put this in". He handed me this stanza form one of Keats' sonnets.

> "To one who has been long in city pent,
> 'Tis very sweet to look into the fair
> And open face to heaven, - - to breathe a prayer
> Full in the face of the blue firmament."

ACKNOWLEDGMENTS

Most of the stories in this book are part of the living folk-lore of the area. Leads and stories have been generously furnished by many people in the area. Without their help these stories could not have been gathered.

Special thanks are due Mr. P. Edwin Clark, the late Mr. E. B. TerBush, Sr., and Mr. Sidney Delaney, of Ellenville; Mr. Kenneth Hasbrouck of New Paltz; Mr. Joe Skepmose, Mr. Johanes Upright, and Mr. Everett Aumich of Rutsonville; Miss Neva Shultis of Woodstock; Messrs. George and Henry Botchford of Woodland Valley; Mr. Richard Atwater and Mr. Martin Rubin of Phoenicia; Mr. John Lindmark of Poughkeepsie; and Judge Roscoe Ellsworth of Port Ewen.

For encouragement and enthusiasm, thanks are due to Mrs. Joan Cortes of Pine Bush who typed the manuscript, Mr. Herman Kondell of Ellenville who supervised the production of the book,

Mr. David Fairbanks, for his hand lettering, and to Mr. Al Sokol for his beautiful layout and design.

And, of course, a final word of thanks to my wife, Leslie, who shared these interests, accompanied me on most of my "visits" and who has been a gentle but severe critic.

This second edition was made possible by the encouragement and assistance of Carol Charles and Sharon van Ivan, both of Ellenville. Their contributions ranged from computer processing to objective criticism. Also, many thanks to Vicki Doyle of the D&H Canal Historical Society for her extra attention in coordinating this project.

PROCEEDS

Proceeds from the sale of this book will be donated to the Delaware & Hudson Canal Historical Society to further their efforts to preserve, protect and perpetuate the history of the D&H Canal, America's first million dollar enterprise. The printing of this edition marks the 100th anniversary of the last boat to navigate the D&H Canal, built in 1828 to haul anthracite coal from Honesdale, Pennsylvania to Kingston, New York to fuel New York City's burgeoning industries. The Society's D&H Canal Museum and mile-long Five Locks Walk, a National Historic Landmark, are located in High Falls, New York.

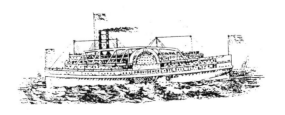

Introduction

Throughout the ages, and among all nations, legends of treasure have excited men's imaginations to dreams of golden ease, Mr. Average Man, leading his "dull life of quiet desperation", has always fancied that to be rich is to be happy. However, it generally takes a lot of work and a long time to get rich and therefore, he feels that happiness is a long way off. The prospect of future reward is not as sharp a spur to action as immediate payment. If one could only become rich overnight, happiness would quickly follow.

With these thoughts in mind, the alchemist of ancient days toiled over steaming flasks and cryptic symbols to discover the Philosopher's Stone, that secret substance which would transmute base metal into gold. Reaching forward through time, the alchemist would find a brother in spirit in the man who buys a sweepstakes ticket, takes a flyer in oil, prospects for minerals in lonely wilds, or more specifically, the man who seeks buried treasure.

The romance of buried treasure lies in the fact that it is a toil-free path to instant wealth. A pot of gold is made available without having to struggle through to the end of the rainbow. Who among us has not dreamed of discovering buried treasure and who does not thrill on reading accounts of its discovery. And so, at heart, we are all Cinderellas seeking instant wealth, that ageless Prince Charming, to transport us immediately from the scullery to the castle.

The Ellenville area of New York State abounds in legends of buried treasure. It is an old area, long settled by the Indians and then by the White Men; and the people have always created their wealth from its ample resources. Their mode of living, their occupations, their trade channels, and their legends have been determined by their heritage and their land; and the greatest single geographic fact in their lives are the great mountain ranges, the Shawangunks and the Catskills.

The Shawangunk Mountains are the most northerly range of the Alleghanies. They start below the Hudson River port of Kingston in Ulster County and run south-westerly through Sullivan and Orange Counties. The range continues through the northern part of New Jersey where it reaches its highest elevation, appropriately enough at High Point, and it continues on into Pennsylvania. There, at the Delaware Water Gap, the range is cut by the Delaware River winding its way to the sea.

Some say, Shawangunk means "Great Wall" in the language of the Leni-Lenape Indians who inhabited the area when the first White Men came; and this "Great Wall" forms the eastern side of the rich Rondout and Mamakating Valleys. The western slopes of the valley are the foothills of the Catskills which grow succeedingly taller as they recede to the jagged horizon which lies in the heart of the Catskill Mountain country.

These valleys form the natural highway between the Hudson and Delaware Rivers, a circumstance recognized by both the Red Man and the White. The ancient Indian trails ran parallel to the Shawangunks connecting these rivers. Later, the Old Mine Road, one of the Nation's oldest highways, over which the lead, zinc, and copper of New Jersey and Pennsylvania was brought to tidewater at Kingston, followed the old trail. Then in the early 1800's, the Delaware and Hudson Canal, which brought such great wealth and activity to these valleys, connected the two great rivers and provided the means by which anthracite, "the stone that burns" was transported from the coal fields in Pennsylvania to the markets of New York. With the development of the railroads, the canal was abandoned and today, U. S. Highway 209 follows the path and performs the function of its predecessors.

The Shawangunk Range is a mighty spine formed by the buckling of the earth's crust in prehistoric times. It is much older than its taller neighbor, the Catskills and entirely different in appearance. From the flat green valleys, first cultivated by the Indians, unannounced by foothills, the sheer cliffs of the Shawangunks rise, a truly great wall. The crest is surprisingly flat, and is covered by gnarled pines huddled close together, stunted by fierce winter winds. From a distance, they appear like a lush green carpet upon which one may walk. Set like jewels along this verdant ridge is a series of blue glacial lakes bearing the wonderful Indian names: Mohonk, Minnewaska, Awosting, and Maratanza.

From a point of vantage, a breathtaking panorama unfolds; to the south, High Point in New Jersey; to the southeast, Storm King and the Highlands of the Hudson; to the east, the Housatonic Mountains of Connecticut; to the northeast, the Berkshires of

Massachusetts and the Green Mountains of Vermont; and to the northwest and west, the rugged peaks and deep valleys of the Catskills fall back in successive planes of purple.

The Catskills are not a single range, and they occupy a wide area. Deep cloves run in all directions cutting off one tall mountain from another; but when viewed from the Hudson River, they present a formidable front known as the Wall of the Manitou. The Manitou were two of the Indian Spirits that lived in the Catskills and in the words of Longfellow:

> "Gitchie Manitou the mighty,
> He, the master of life, was painted
> As an egg, with points projecting
> To the four winds of the heavens,
> "'Everywhere is the Great Spirit," - -
> Was the meaning of the symbol.
> Mitchie Manitou the mighty,
> He, the dreadful Spirit of Evil,
> As a serpent was depicted,
> As Kenabeck, the great serpent.
> "Very crafty, very cunning,
> Is the creeping Spirit of Evil,' - -
> Was the meaning of the symbol."

Catskill derives from the Dutch, "Kaat" meaning wild cat and "Kil" meaning narrow body of water. Thus the Catskills are the Mountains of Wild Cat Creek. Not nearly as pretty as the Indian, "Onteora", the Mountains of the Sky.

The forbidding Catskills were not settled by the Dutch nor explored by them and even the Indians gave them wide berth. The wild cats, the lack of natural trails, and the scarcity of land level enough to cultivate, all combined to preserve the splendor of the area until the early 1800's when the voracious Tanneries arrived to gobble up the Hemlocks which covered the slopes in a heavy blue-green blanket. Aside from these natural obstacles to exploration, the Dutch as well as the Indians believed that supernatural forces and beings were at work in the Catskills; and of course, they could cite the strange case of Rip Van Winkle as proof.

The area was first described in 1609 by Hendrick Hudson who marveled at the mountains as he sailed up the river which now bears his name. Unverified tradition tells us that by 1614, a trading post was established at Rondout in the present city of Kingston. The first permanent residents headed by dashing Thomas Chambers arrived in 1653 and by 1661 Governor Stuyvesant granted a charter to Wildwyck. In 1664 English rule succeeded the Dutch and even though the Dutch again ruled briefly in 1673, during which time Kingston was called Swanenburgh, the growth of the area was steady. By this time there were settlements in Niew Dorp (Hurley), Rosendale, Rochester and Marbletown, and by 1671 French Hugenots had settled New Paltz. So it was, in a very short span of time, prophetic of our country's role as a melting pot, the Indians, Dutch, French, and English with their diverse languages, customs and cultural heritages, were intermingled. This amalgamation was almost complete by the time of the Revolutionary War. And by that time, the people of the Shawangunks and the Catskills had begun creating their legends.

Dutch Gold / 1

Early View of New Amsterdam

In 1638, William Kieft, the newly appointed Director, arrived to take charge of the settlement at New Amsterdam. He was a man ill fitted for the job. He started out in life as a merchant and soon ended this phase of his career in bankruptcy.

His first service in foreign lands was in Turkey. He was sent there by a group of people that had raised a sum of money to ransom their Christian friends who were held by the Turks. He was only partially successful in his mission. Some prisoners were left behind. Back in Holland, some said that he left those people in bondage deliberately and kept the ransom money.

At the time of his arrival, New Amsterdam was in desperate condition. The fort was open on every side, the guns were dismounted and all the buildings were in need of repair. Only one of the three windmills was operating and five farms of the Dutch West

India Company were deserted. The trading monopoly which the States General, the governing body of Holland, had granted to the Dutch West India Company was being evaded and firearms were being sold to the Indians.

Director Kieft immediately took firm steps to establish the discipline and morale of the settlement. Work hours were fixed, and fighting, lewdness, rebellion, theft, perjury, calumny, and "all other immoralities" were forbidden by edict. The sale of liquor and tobacco was regulated.

Under his ruthless hand, the colony began to prosper and this prosperity gave such confidence to Kieft that he felt that he could do no wrong. As the fort and the garrison were rendered into an effective defense, the emboldened Kieft demanded tribute from the Indians. He claimed that he had orders from Holland to exact a tribute of coins, furs, and wampum from the Indians. This policy was resented and evaded by the Indians and was the first step in the tragic deterioration of relationships between the grasping Director and the previously friendly Indians.

In 1640 some of the livestock of David De Vries was stolen and the Raritan Indians were blamed. It was later proven that these cattle were stolen by the Dutch; but an expedition was sent out in July against the Raritans. Several of the Indians were killed and their crops were destroyed. There then began a long series of bloody incidents as the Dutch attempted to exact their tribute. The Tappan Indians, "wondered how the sachem at the fort dared to exact such things from them." "He must be a very shabby fellow: he had come to live in their land when they had not invited him, and now came to deprive them of their corn for nothing."

Meanwhile in Rensselaerswyck, where the patroon Kiliaen Van Rensselaer had established a colony in 1629, the Mohawk tribe of the Iroquois Indians were being sold firearms. Their hereditary enemies were the Algonquin tribes of the lower Hudson Valley and Long Island. Early in 1643, about 90 Mohawks armed with guns obtained at Rensselaerswyck, embarked on a war party against the Algonquin tribes in the Hudson Valley. About 70 Algonquins were killed in the first skirmishes and the rest of the Indians, although alienated from the Dutch, came down to the area around Fort Amsterdam where they felt they would be safer.

The more moderate people in Fort Amsterdam felt that this would be a wonderful opportunity to ease the hard feelings and patch up the old feud between them and the Algonquins. Director Kieft, aided by several hot headed counselors decided, contrary to popular opinion, to take advantage of the helpless condition of the Algonquins. On the night of February 25, 1643, two troops set out from Fort Amsterdam against two separate encampments of the river Indians. The first party, under the direction of Rodolf, slaughtered 80 Indians of both sexes and of all ages at Pavonia, (Jersey City). At the same time at Corlaer's Book, the party led by Adriaensen massacred 40 more Indians. For sheer savagery and brutality, these treacherous attacks have never been surpassed by either Indian or White man, and the triumphant soldiers returned in a Roman procession with 30 captives and also with the heads of many of their victims. Eleven of the local tribes rose up against the Dutch and all of the outlying settlements were destroyed. Many of the early settlers in such places as Long Island, Brooklyn, Westchester and New Haven were killed.

Through the efforts of David De Vries later in the year, a few of the Long Island tribes were placated. However, the tribes in the Hudson Valley continued to take a toll of Dutch lives. Trade came to a virtual standstill and all thoughts of further settlement had to be abandoned. The early prosperity of Kieft's regime vanished. Before the year ended, Anne Hutchinson who had fled the intolerance of the Puritans in New England to seek refuge in the Hudson Valley, fell victim to this senseless war.

The most moderate of the Dutch, David De Vries, the only Dutchman who could walk among the Indians unarmed, became fed up with the bloody policies of Kieft. De Vries had lost all of his possessions in the fighting and despite all his efforts to achieve peace, he was constantly thwarted by the Director. In his final interview with Kieft, he shouted the awful prophesy, "The murders in which you have shed so much innocent blood will yet be avenged upon your head." With these words De Vries the peacemaker left New Amsterdam forever.

For the next two years it was not safe for any Dutchman to leave Fort Amsterdam unarmed or unaccompanied. The suffering settlers, thoroughly disgusted with Kieft's administration, wrote to Holland asking that he be dismissed and replaced. By the end of 1644, it was determined to recall Kieft but no successor was named. Fresh troops arrived early in 1645 and by the spring, the Indians again renewed attempts at peace. After many negotiations, peace with the Algonquins was concluded. Now, for the first time, Kieft went up the Hudson River to the trading post at Fort Orange. Here, adjacent to the buildings of Kiliaen Van Rensselaier, peace for the entire area was assured in a treaty with the Mohawk Indians and here was set the first encounter with the treasures of the Catskills.

In arranging the treaty of peace with the Mohawks and other local tribes, an Indian interpreter named Agheroense, who was well known to the Christians as well as to the Indians, was called to assist. All of the chiefs gathered on one side of the clearing and on the other side were the officials of Rensselaerswyck, Director Kieft and Adriaen Van der Donck, Doctor of Laws and historian for the colony.

One morning during the negotiations, the sharp eyed Van der Donck noticed a very peculiar event. In his words, Agheroense, "who lodged in the director's house, came down stairs and in the presence of the director and myself sat down, and began stroking and painting his face. The director, observing the operation, asked me to inquire of the Indian what substance he was using, which he handed to me, and I handed to the director. After he had examined it attentively, he judged, from its weight and greasy lustre, that it must be some valuable mineral. So we commuted with the Indian for it, in order to see what it was. We acted with it as we best could, under the direction of a certain Johannes la Montagne, doctor in medicine, and counselor in New Netherland, a man of intelligence, who had some knowledge or science in these matters. To be brief; it was put into a crucible, and after it had been thought to be long enough in the fire, it was taken out, and two pieces of gold were found in it, which were both judged to be worth about three guilders. This proof was at first kept very still."

Back at New Amsterdam, where the exultant Kieft, Van der Donck and la Montagne kept their golden secret, preparations were under way to get more of this valuable ore. An officer and several men, guided by the Indians, were led to a hole where Agheroense had obtained his decorative ore. The party brought back a bucketful and it was again placed in the crucible of la Montagne and again the crucible yielded molten gold.

Further samples were obtained and put in charge of Arendt Corssen, one of the first traders on the Delaware and he was dispatched by Kieft to Holland in the winter of 1645. There was no ship at Manhattan so Corssen went to New Haven where he embarked about Christmas on an 80 ton vessel. That winter was one of the earliest and sharpest since the settlement of New England and the harbor was frozen. With difficulty, the harbor was cleared of ice and the ship finally got to sea. But the winter storms were too much for the frail boat and it foundered at sea. Director Kieft's messenger, Arendt Corssen and all others on board - - and the gold - - were never heard of again.

By this time, Kieft had learned that several of the colonists had appealed for his dismissal at Amsterdam and he learned that Pegleg Peter Stuyvesant was appointed as his successor. The imperious Stuyvesant after many delays, arrived in 1647. He was an old soldier who had lost his leg in a wild charge at Curacao and it was immediately apparent to the expectant colonists that their hopes for a more liberal director were not realized.

Two of the burghers, Kuyter and Melyn insisted upon an examination of Kieft's policy so that a report could be returned to the States General in Holland informing them of his incompetence and cruelty. Stuyvesant realized the justice of their cause but he did not want to set a precedent whereby the common citizenry could impeach the authority of the director. So he in turn arrested Kuyter and Melyn and imprisoned them. After mock trial, he banished them from the colony for rebellion and treachery and they were returned to Holland as political prisoners on the same ship that was returning the triumphant ex-director, William Kieft, to his native land.

The exultant Kieft had taken on board, on this same triumphant ship that carried his political enemies home in disgrace, a large quantity of the golden ore of the Catskills. As the ship approached the coast of England, the satisfied Kieft reviewed his life. After a lifetime of adventures in the maelstroms of commerce, among barbarous Turks and savage Indians, he was going home rich! He had survived the rigors of the New World and had made it yield its most precious treasure. He was a jubilant man.

As Kieft's ship, the Princess, swung into the Bristol channel for its first stop on the way home, it struck a rock and soon the towering breakers of the rugged coast of Wales began to demolish the ship. They were trapped beyond help by the powerful seas and as death approached, the conscience stricken Kieft turned to his enemies Kuyter and Melyn, "Friends, I have been unjust towards you - - can you forgive me?" By morning, the ship had completely disintegrated. Kuyter and Melyn clinging to pieces of the wreckage were tossed up on shore. Kieft battered by the sea, found no buoyant wreckage to sustain him. As he weakened, De Vries' awful prophecy reverberated through his mind, "The murders in which you have shed so much innocent blood will yet be avenged upon your head." With these words ringing in his ears, the watery grave of Arendt Corssen opened to receive Kieft and his treasure.

Peter Stuyvesant

Dutch Silver /2

The summer of 1646 witnessed two important events along the Hudson River. First, Kiliaen van Rensselaer, the first patroon of Rensselaerswyck died, and secondly, Director Kieft issued a patent to the Katskill mountain lands to Cornelius van Slyck of "Breuckelen". The patent to van Slyck was for "the land of Katskill, lying on the River Mauritius, there to plant, with his associates, a colonie according to the freedoms and exemptions of New Netherland." This extensive patent was granted to van Slyck for the great services that he had done "this country, as well in the making of peace as in the ransoming of prisoners, and it being proper that such notorious services should not remain unacknowledged." In granting this patent, Director Kieft set aside the claims of the patroon of Rensselaerswyck for this land and indeed, a patroon's claim had been formerly denied in legal proceedings in 1644.

The heir to Rensselaerswyck, Johannes van Rensseslaer was a minor at his father's death and Brandt van Slechtenhorst was appointed director until Johannes came of age. Since Kiliaen van Rensselaer had founded his colony in 1630, he had reigned as supreme as a feudal baron. He was subject to no laws on this side of the Atlantic and his tenants were as subject to his whims as were the serfs of the Middle Ages. Not only did they owe a portion of their crops to him but they were not allowed to trade without his permission. Here was sowed the groundwork that culminated in the Down Rent Wars which were not settled until the middle of the 19th Century.

At his death, Kiliaen van Rensselaer's colony was the most prosperous of all the Dutch settlements. By trading in firearms, the shrewd patroon had avoided all trouble with the Indians and the growing prosperity of his colony placed it in constant conflict with authorities at the foot of the river in New Amsterdam. Brandt van Slechtenhorst, "a person of stubborn and headstrong temper" was determined to conduct the affairs of Rensselaerswyck according to the policies set down by the dead patroon.

In July 1648, the recently arrived Stuyvesant came up to Fort Orange and attempted to stop the trade in firearms which centered at nearby Rensselaerswyck. Director Stuyvesant ordered van Slechtenhorst to cease the illicit trade in firearms and also warned him against erecting any buildings close to Fort Orange and, in turn, van Slechtenhorst accused Stuyvesant of behaving as if he were patroon of Rensselaerswyck. Disregarding Stuyvesant's orders, van Slechtenhorst continued the trade and built several more houses within pistol shot of Fort Orange.

To make matters worse, early in 1649 van Slechtenhorst in flagrant disregard of Kieft's patent to van Slyck and of the express orders of Stuyvesant, procured title from the Indians to the Katskill lands. With this accomplished, he then began to rent the lands to tenants who were subject to all the regulations of the other farmers of Rensselaerswyck. When Stuyvesant learned of these deeds, which he considered gross insubordination, he was furious. The tide of events at Fort Amsterdam prevented Stuyvesant from acting immediately but the passage of time did not cool his anger. Stuyvesant resolved to take action and his determination was reinforced by the directors of the West India Company, who specifically ordered Stuyvesant to prohibit any settlements there by tenants holding patents issued by the authorities at Rensselaerswyck.

The situation grew more strained as the settlement continued. The events which prevented Stuyvesant from taking decisive action were concerned with the encroachment of the English in the outlying areas of New Netherland. Stuyvesant decided to raise a force to hold back the English and a subsidy was levied against the colony of Rensselaerswyck. Van Slechtenhorst came down to New Amsterdam to protest. Not only were his protests put aside but Stuyvesant, the man with the wooden leg and the iron will, threw van Slechtenhorst into jail at Fort Amsterdam. The sputtering van Slechtenhorst languished in the dingy Fort Amsterdam jail for four months and all of his pleas and protests to Stuyvesant were in vain. In September of 1651, he managed to bribe, "a schipper" who was sailing up the river and the proud Brandt van Slechtenhorst sneaked aboard and was smuggled back to Rensselaerswyck. When Stuyvesant learned about this, his fury mounted to greater heights and when the "'schipper" returned to Fort Amsterdam, he was arrested and fined 250 guilders. However, since van Slechtenhorst had promised to indemnify him, he shrugged the fine off and went on his way.

The real reason for van Slechtenhorst's audacity was that prior to his imprisonment, one of the tenants to whom he had granted a lease in the Katskills had moved in, built a house, and began to farm the lands. The daughter of this farmer found a very heavy stone one day in the fields and this stone contained silver. Van Slechtenhorst learned of this and his imagination soared to think of the great value of the land that he had acquired. However, the constant shadow of Stuyvesant hovered in the background for Stuyvesant was determined that this land would not become part of Rensselaerswyck. The prospect of untold riches in silver was the thorn that goaded Brandt van Slechtenhorst to his reckless disregard of Stuyvesant's authority. He was safe at Rensselaerswyck but in great danger of recapture and unknown punishment from Stuyvesant, if he ventured down to the silver bearing lands of the Katskills. He therefore informed his son Gerrit of the silver ore and instructed him to find the farm and obtain additional ore.

As Gerrit approached the farm which was located in a deep clove in the Katskills, the threatening grey skies opened and a heavy rain began to fall. As the rain rose in intensity from shower, to storm, to cloud burst, the mountain stream along which the farmhouse was located, rose thirty feet to a frothy torrent. The farmhouse was swept away and all the people, cattle, and horses were lost. Gerrit van Slechtenhorst, who was an excellent swimmer, alone managed to survive, and with the disappearance of that farmhouse and its occupants, went the only hope of finding the silver of the Katskills.

Many have sought this treasure and none have found it except perhaps Isaac Diamond two centuries later. Diamond was gathering nuts in the forest near Woodstock. Next to a deep hole, he came upon a small stone heavy for its size. He took the stone home and before he could have it assayed and act upon the information that it contained silver, two years had passed. He set out to find the spot where he made his discovery but the most intensive searches that he frequently made during the rest of his life, could never again locate the deep hole next to which the silver was found. The succeeding generations carried on his search as ours does. The silver has yet to be found.

Legend of Tongoras /3

After the signing of the treaty of peace between Holland and England in February, 1674, New Netherlands passed from Dutch sovereignty. The new English governor, Governor Andros, changed the old settlement's name from Swanenburgh back to Kingston. It was called Swanenburgh in honor of the flagship of the Dutch Admiral, Evertsen, whose fleet liberated New Netherlands from the English only one year previously. One of Governor Andros' first acts was to send a small garrison of soldiers to the Kingston area to maintain peace. The Indians were no longer a serious threat and many of them were of assistance to the tiny garrison.

One of the most cooperative Indians was Tongoras, a chieftan of the Esopus tribe. The area known as Tongore in the Township of Olive still bears a modified version of his name. Although Tongoras was a helpful man, with great sway over his fellow Indians, he was not entirely without thought of recompense for his favors. Moreover, he was sufficiently sophisticated to demand the coin of the King's Realm for his efforts, not the wampum or the other trifles which passed for currency among the border Indians.

Apparently his services were in demand and his reward great. In addition, he was a thrifty soul and he accumulated a large amount of hard money. These riches he planned to take with him to the Happy Hunting Ground when the Great Spirit called. When he died he was buried legend tells us, in the flats along the Esopus Creek and with him was interred his fortune in gold and silver coins. This legend has led to many searches, all unsuccessful.

Perhaps the treasure now lies buried for all time under the bottom of the Ashokan Reservoir which was formed by damming the Esopus Creek in that area or perhaps he did take his treasure to the Happy Hunting Ground.

A Story
of the Ashokan /4

Building the Ashokan Dam

The Ashokan Reservoir which hides beneath its surface the treasure of Tongoras, also hides seven abandoned villages. Two thousand people had to move out of the area now submerged, according to a 1916 Board of Water Supply publication. Thirty two cemeteries had to be relocated and 2800 bodies had to be reinterred. In this process a very singular discovery was made and this discovery led to one of the few tales of the area in which the treasure sought, was found. It proved to be a treasure more precious than seekers after treasure dream about, and it illustrates one of the rare instances where base motives did not achieve base results. The treasure found was life itself, and the singular discovery was an empty coffin in one of the cemeteries.

Many years ago, in the Township of Olive, there lived a very prosperous farmer who had a lovely daughter. This young girl was afflicted by a strange ailment which manifested itself in the form of fainting spells. These fainting spells were frequently brought on by excitement or by nervous tension and the poor girl suffered greatly from them. Usually her spell would last only a few minutes.

Despite this handicap, her graciousness and beauty made her very popular among the younger people in the neighborhood. In time, one of the youths proposed to her and she accepted. The family was elated by the news and great preparations were made for the wedding. A beautiful white wedding gown was made and many precious family heirlooms were gotten out to be worn with it. Among these heirlooms were rings, a necklace with locket, and a pair of earrings.

People were invited from the surrounding communities and huge quantities of food were made ready. As the feverish preparations which are so typical of these joyous occasions mounted to their highest pitch on the day before the wedding, the young bride had one of her spells. This time she did not come out of it quickly and the doctor was called. All of his efforts to revive her were in vain and finally he pronounced her dead.

Tragedy striking in the midst of festivity produces the darkest gloom of all. The wedding guests became mourners and the groom's despair was bottomless. The bride's grief-stricken family prepared her for burial in the costume in which she was to be married, jewels and all. She was carried to the cemetery in a despondent procession with four of her young farmer friends acting as pallbearers and the stunned group saw her coffin interred. They departed with the knell of the shoveled clods of earth thumping on the coffin lid, still echoing in their ears.

Later that day, two young pallbearers who had been very good friends of the bride, began discussing the uncertainty of life and the necessity of enjoying it while one lived. These two boys were farmers, unhappy with their lot in life, and anxious to go to the city to do the great things young men dream about. Apparently the same thought occurred to both of them and they carefully sounded each other out. They learned that they were in accord, They reasoned that it was foolish, useless, and wasteful to allow those jewels to be buried with the dead who had no use for them, when they, the living, needed them so desperately.

The rising moon found the young men shoveling out the loose earth from the new grave. Then came the hollow sound as the shovels hit the coffin lid. Finally enough was cleared so that they could get down and lift the lid off the coffin. The diffused moonlight cast a faint light on that ghoulish scene. The beautiful bride in white stared heavenward with wide open but unseeing eyes. Those eyes which accused the men no matter which way they turned. At last, conquering both terror and conscience, they removed the earrings and the necklace from the pallid, limp body. The ring was another matter. It wouldn't come off. In terror and panic one of the men gave a rough, sudden tug. The ring came off and with it, some skin. The hand began to bleed and suddenly the girl sat up.

The men shrieked. They didn't know whether they were sane or mad - - living or dead. The pandemonium within them

34

finally subsided as the truth of the situation penetrated; and wrapping the shivering girl in their coats, they brought her back to her astounded family.

Well, that wedding finally did take place and the bride lived to a ripe old age after raising a fine family. When she died, she was buried in that same cemetery in another grave. When she was disturbed a second time by the coming of the Ashokan Reservoir she did not sit up and now she sleeps forever in the Mt. Evergreen Cemetery in Woodstock.

Legend of Unapois /5

Tongoras, the Esopus Chieftan, hoarded his money and died with it. Another Indian named Unapois sought to share his wealth and unfortunately, his altruism led him to an untimely end. Let us remember that this is a legend, not a parable, and proceed with this point in mind.

It seems that one day Unapois, a brave of the Leni-Lenape Indians, noticed the gold wedding ring on the hand of the wife of an early settler in the Shawangunk area. Unapois scornfully asked her, "Why do you wear such trifles?" The woman's husband, standing near, overheard this remark and, according to an earlier written record, said, "If you will procure for me such trifles, I will reward you with many things suitable to you." Unapois replied, "I know of a mounain filled with such metal." The settler then offered to Unapois the following: red and blue cloth, white lead, looking glasses, bodkins, and needles. He further offered to provide an escort to the mountain filled with gold. Unapois accepted the presents and declined the escort, promising to return with a sample of the precious metal.

Keeping to his word, Unapois returned in several days with a lump of ore as large as his fist. From this huge nugget, enough gold was extracted to make several rings and bracelets. The elated settler had visions of a life free from the burden of struggling with the soil for a meagre living. He saw in his mind's eye a vast estate with slaves which few in the area could afford to do his work, a fine stone house with formal gardens, and a coach with a fine team of horses. The settler promised Unapois many valuable presents if he would reveal the location of the mountain. Unapois agreed but first requested a delay of a few days so that he might visit his family and his tribe from whom he had been absent during his trip to the secret mountain. He was given more presents to cement the bargain and in a short time, his tribesmen beheld this warrior bearing gifts. The chief questioned him. Unapois, alas, was a boaster. It was his boast to the settler's wife that brought the entire matter to pass, and true to his nature, he boastfully explained his plans to the chief.

Now it so happened that these Indians were not without legends of their own. One of their legends explained that their people were passing through a period of punishment for an offense that they had given the Great Spirit. This punishment was the plague-like invasion of the white man who was taking their land and killing their game. Soon, the Great Spirit, would smile upon them with favor once again and the land which was rightfully theirs would be returned to them. The game would come back and the white man would leave.

Therefore, they wished to preserve the location of the gold mine until the land was again theirs. Then they could without fear, adorn themselves with the ever gleaming metal as their ancestors once did. The chief called together the elders of the tribe and they sat in council to consider Unapois actions. After much deliberation, they decided that he was a traitor to his people. The settler waited in vain for his return. Unapois had been put to death by his tribesmen and the location of his bones is as much of a secret as the location of the gold mine.

Claudius Smith /6

Perhaps the preceding anecdotes do not qualify as real tales of buried treasure in the mind of the reader. They have none of the romance of the ill-gotten gains of such pirates as Captain Kidd or Jean La Fitte, none of the thrilling elements of the chase, nor are there allusions to faded hand drawn maps. Nowhere was there reference to the rattle of ancient flintlocks, nor in the end was the dastardly villain led to the gallows, "with nimble feet to dance upon the air." Here then is an authentic tale of the Shawangunks which contains these elements.

During the Revolutionary War, the Shawangunk area was an exposed frontier. The last outposts of the patriots, or Whigs as they were then called, were the settlements along the Rondout Valley. The history of that period is filled with the terrors and massacres that befell these fighters for liberty. None but the student or local resident knows of the wanton burning of Kingston, the tragic Battle of the Minisink, the pathetic Fantine Kill massacre, or the destruction of Warwarsing to name but a few of the incidents. Along this Rondout frontier, the Mohawk Indians, instigated by the British, and led by able leaders like Brandt, killed and looted. The British strategy was aimed more at tying up scarce colonial troops than at specific military objectives. It was this constant harrying by the Mohawks that led to General Sullivan's campaign which broke the back of Indian power in the area at the important Battle of Oriskany.

If the Indians were feared, the Tories were loathed. These Tories were citizens who remained loyal to the crown and they acted as spies and informers. Frequently, they masqueraded as Indians and descended upon their unsuspecting neighbors, killing and stealing, motivated more by avarice and jealousy, than by loyalty to the King of England.

The most infamous of all the Tories in the Shawangunk area was Claudius Smith. He was a man whose antisocial tendencies were apparent before the war. He was a convicted cattle thief and public records show that he was sent to jail in Kingston. He was transferred to the jail in Goshen from which he later escaped. His father is reported to have encouraged his thieving propensities; but his mother, dismayed by his early deeds, prophesied, "Claudius, some day you'll die like a trooper's horse - - with your shoes on."

After his escape, Smith gathered about him a band of highwaymen, hoodlums, thieves, and every other type of outlaw. They roamed the area east of the Shawangunk Mountains looting, murdering and pillaging. His most frequent victims were prominent Whigs in Orange County, and when pursuit got too hot, he withdrew to areas of British control at Stony Point or Fort Lee.

Claudius Smith was a capable leader and if his abilities had been combined with the fine character typical of so many colonial leaders, history would have a different tale to tell. Even so there are tales of a definite Robin Hood flavor which have come down. One tells of a poor woman who tried to borrow money from a local miser so that she could help her husband who was a prisoner of war of the British. Claudius Smith hearing of the miser's refusal, robbed him of his money and gave it to the woman.

As the war progressed, his activities became more and more daring. He was joined by his two sons, Richard and James and their band of brigands became in fact, a guerilla army. Smith became a constant threat to the unprotected rear areas. He brought about his own downfall when he assassinated an important colonial officer, Major Strong. Governor Clinton offered a large reward for the capture of Smith and his sons. Evidently they felt that they had gone too far and they fled to Long Island. They were followed there by a party led by Major John Brush and one night, Claudius Smith was surprised in his sleep at the house of a Tory friend and captured. He was brought back under heavy guard and placed in irons in the same Goshen jail from which he had escaped to lead his reign of terror. After a trial he was sentenced to death on June 13, 1779.

As he stood on the gallows, he stooped and removed his shoes with great deliberation. In reply to a question about this act, he repeated his mother's prophesy and explained, "I want to make her out a liar." These were his last words. His son, Richard succeeded his father but lacked his qualities of leadership. He was driven to Canada with several members of his gang. Nothing more was heard of James. Nor was any of the tremendous booty that the band had acquired, located.

In 1804, some of Smith's descendants, probably grandchildren, came down from Canada armed this time only with instructions, instructions for locating the loot hidden in the mountains. All that they found was a cache of rusty muskets.

In 1824, the descendants of another member of the band, Edward Roblin came down from Canada with old maps and written instructions. They searched long and well and found nothing of value. Years afterward, a man by the name of Wood was leaning on his cane in the village green of Goshen. The cane gave way under him as it slipped down into a hollow area under the turf. Shovels were employed and a skeleton was unearthed. Investigation established that these bones were the remains of Claudius Smith who had been buried in the shadow of the old gallows.

Crowds of curious came and carried away portions of the skeleton as souveniers. Orrin Ensign, the village blacksmith, made knife handles of some of the bones. These attractive and useful instruments found great favor, brought high prices, and functioned well through the years.

And so ends the story of Claudius Smith, who himself provided the only buried treasure to recall his days on earth, and who finally ended up by being of some use to the citizens of Orange County.

Tory Treasure /7

"Esopus (Kingston) is the nursery of almost every villain in the country." So wrote British General Vaughan to his superior, Sir Harry Clinton, in the report of his burning of Kingston. By villain, General Vaughn meant patriot and those few people who were not villains in General Vaughan's estimation, were Tories. These Tories, you may be sure, were quite unpopular in Kingston during the Revolutionary War and when feelings ran high, to be unpopular was to be unsafe, and so, many of the Tories fled. One of the refuges was the Catskill Mountains which had not been penetrated to any extent at that time. Many of these Tories found refuge in the vicinity of High Point and some of the more adventurous found their way to the area around Woodstock.

One of these Tories was a wealthy man who managed to take with him most of his family's possessions. Among these items were a fine silver tea set, the family silverware, and he also carried his personal wealth in the form of several bags of gold. He fled

Kingston in a style befitting his position attended by a young slave boy. When he reached the area beyond Woodstock, he apparently felt that his possessions were slowing up his movements. He also felt that to have such wealth would make him the prey of any highwaymen who chanced upon him. Somewhere along the road between Bearsville and Coopers Lake, he made a decision. He decided to bury his treasure.

His slave boy dug a deep hole and into this hole were placed his fine silverware and his gold. Before covering up the hole, he decided that he had taken several natural means to conceal his treasure but yet, it was not quite safe enough. He decided to invoke the supernatural for additional safety. In what better way was there, than to create a haunt or a "han't," as they are called in the mountains. A "han't" is the spirit of a murdered person and as he looked at his slave boy, he realized that here was a way of doubly guarding his secret. The little slave was the only living person who knew where the treasure was buried and there came to the Tory's mind, the old pirate adage, "dead men tell no tales." Moreover, this dead man would then be the "han't" to frighten people away from the vicinity and so, according to the descendants of the fighters for liberty who live in that area, the same blackness of heart which led the man to become a Tory, led him to murder a poor defenseless slave who was buried with his master's treasure.

In the end, the irony was complete. The Tory never returned for his treasure and generations of people travelling the road between Bearsville and Coopers Lake have seen the "han't" or have had their horses shy at the sight of him. For those foolish people who are not afraid of han'ts, the treasure lies waiting.

44

Lost Silver Mine /8

The Bettman Archive

Just prior to the Revolutionary War, while Claudius Smith was till pursuing his early career as a petty criminal and cattle thief, and the causes which divided Whig and Tory were still smoldering, two men were engaged in a secret, lucrative pursuit, albeit an honest one. They were working a silver mine, the location of which, tradition can do no better than tell us was somewhere in the Shawangunk Mountains. These men were led to the mine by friendly Indians and in order to keep their secret, they worked only at night. They took many precautions to see that they were not followed and they were careful to leave no trail. To dispose of the ore, they made long mysterious journeys to unknown destinations, or so it seemed to their neighbors who shared none of their confidences.

This cautious behavior sprang from prudence, not from any antisocial tendency on the part of these two miners. Evidence of this is the fact that these men ceased their mine activities and joined the Patriots Army when the Revolutionary War broke out. Before leaving, they drew a large flat stone over the mouth of the mine, covered the area with foliage and marked a clump of trees which stood close by. They shook hands and pledged to one another that they would not reveal their secret to any other.

The war's toll was heavy. One of the miners was killed. The other who left his family behind almost lost trace of his kin. They were in constant danger from the Indians and Tories since they lived on the exposed frontier. This family, after beholding the atrocities which befell their neighbors, lacking the head of the household for protection, finally gave up and fled. After the war the surviving soldier returned to look for his family. He found that they had fled, and he immediately began to search for them. He found them after several years. They were in desperate need and he was hard pressed to provide the necessities of life for them. Nine years passed before he was able to leave his family and return to the Shawangunks to look for his silver mine. He found that during the intervening years, the Indians had burned the marked trees and obliterated the landmarks. He could not find his mine, nor has anyone else to this day.

Old 99 /9

The preceding legend is unusual among the ones that tradition and old writings have passed down to us. It has none of the attraction of the others in that it cannot be related directly to any definite area. There are no old family names of long departed residents. Nothing specific is mentioned, nor are the Indians who gave up the secret identified. Nor does it seem believable that the mine could not again be located by a man who had visited it so many times. In short, it is not the sort of a story which can be believed, nor does it capture the imagination.

Why then should we tell it? The answer lies in its outline. If any one variety of legend is typical of the area, it is the one where some friendly Indian showed some friendly white man, a mine or a treasure under any one of a variety of circumstances; but later on, depending upon the variation of the theme, the white man can no longer locate the hidden bonanza.

This outline is almost as definite as the outline of certain works of art, like the sonnet or symphony in which the artist working within that frame, creates endless varieties. In time, this form dies because no new expression can be found within its framework and in retrospect, certain works represent the greatest expression of that form. To many, the sonnets of Shakespeare or the symphonies of Beethoven fall into this category.

The legend which was the ultimate within our framework of buried treasure, is Old 99's Cave. This one legend is still a living force in the Shawangunks. Young men still explore the mountains never letting a crevice or a cave go uninvestigated, still hoping to rediscover Old 99's Cave. Indeed, as the author writes this legend, he wonders what lies beyond a sharp turn after the entrance to a certain cave near the crest of the range facing the Hudson. Waist deep water and uncertain footing makes further investigation dangerous, that is until spring when the proper equipment can be brought up to assist in getting by this barrier.

Old 99, Neopakintic, was a Warwarsing chief and was supposed to have been the sole survivor of the 99th tribe of the Leni-Lenape Indians. After the Revolutionary War, he enjoyed great local fame as a hunter and a trapper. However, he engaged in these activities only in the winter. When summer came, he would relax and enjoy his idleness with his friends. One of these friends was Benny Depuy, a man noted for his laziness. However, Benny did fish and hunt occasionally and he liked to exchange stories. Over the years, the Indian and Benny became fast cronies and Neopakintic knew that he could trust Benny.

One day, Old 99 told Benny of his trust in him and he told him that he would show Benny a sight which he would never forget. This sight, he told Benny, was one which Old 99 would not even show to his own brother, He asked Benny to accompany him on his next trip into the mountains and Benny agreed.

They started up the mountain from a path leaving Port Ben on the old Delaware and Hudson Canal. They clambered up over loose rocks and fallen trees until they came to the dry bed of a mountain stream. Here the Indian blindfolded Benny and they struggled up the stream bed, taking first this branch and then another. They fought their way upward for about an hour as near as Benny could estimate. When the blindfold was removed, they were at the base of a high ledge of rocks, similar to hundreds of other ledges in the area.

The muscular old Indian rolled aside a boulder and a passageway which ran directly into the cliff was disclosed. Old 99 told Benny to hang on behind him by his shirt as the Indian led the way in the black cave. Benny was a superstitious man and he expected to be carried away by the goblins. He was genuinely sorry that he came along on this adventure.

Then old 99 lit a candle and they found themselves in a large stone vault which had been hewn from solid rock. On the floor were rugs, so rich and deep that their boots gave no sound. Costly tapestries hung from the side of the cavern and along the walls were precious vases and other rare and beautiful objects. Old 99 strode to a corner and opened a large wooden chest. In a voice muffled by the gloom, Neopakintic, last survivor of the 99th tribe of the Leni-Lenape Indians, said to Benny Depuy, "Look into this chest". Benny crossed the cavern and looking past the lighted candle into the chest, beheld a sight which was to haunt him for the rest of his life. There in the chest, glistened heaps upon heaps of gold and silver coins, and precious stones. Old 99 raked his hands back and forth through these shining treasures as Benny Depuy stood, wide-eyed and mouth agape. Then the Indian said, "Let us go" and he led Benny out of the cave. The boulder was rolled back into place and Benny was again blindfolded. They descended slowly as Benny, blindfolded, hung onto the Indian. At last, the blindfold was removed and Benny found himself on the path back to Port Ben.

Shortly thereafter, Old 99 disappeared. He was never seen again. Benny waited to make sure that Old 99, whom he feared, would not return and finally convinced of this, he set out to find Old 99's Cave. For the rest of his life, he searched without success. It has never been found. The story is still believed and each generation gives forth a romantic few who continue to search.

To those skeptics who wonder how plush rugs, rich tapestries, rare vases, and other treasures of alien culture became the secret treasure of the 99th tribe of the Leni-Lenape Indians, there is an explanation. The stirring adventures of Captain Kidd which follow later in the book, will clear up this mystery.

"Old Ninety Nine's Cave", a book by Elizabeth Gray, published in 1909, was probably responsible for keeping this legend alive. In this fanciful novel, fact and fiction are so intertwined that it is impossible to tell one from the other. The book shows actual photographs of people who lived in Ellenville but gives them names of characters in the book. All geographic names and locations are accurate with the exception of Napanoch which is called Nootwyck and Ellenville, which is called Elmdale.

The plot is a quaint specimen of Victorian writing in which all the villains have hearts as black as coal and these dastardly scoundrels lurking behind fierce moustaches, had nary a redeeming trait. On the other hand the people that were good, were very very good and trod constantly in the paths of virtue. No coincidence is too remote but helps the plot along and no evil event occurs, without the victim having a presentiment of the impending catastrophe.

The authoress, Miss Gray, was a nurse and therefore, virtually every protagonist in the book spends at least two chapters on his death bed, victims of all the horrible diseases known to man, including leprosy. Nevertheless, virtue triumphs, Old 99's cave is rediscovered and in it, is a rich vein of gold. In no time, Nootwyck (Napanoch, present population 2,000) is transformed into a thriving metropolis of 90,000 happy souls, complete with colleges, factories, technical institutes, and railroad terminals.

One complication remains to be cleared up. The heroine has married the wrong man. He is a fine gentleman, but nevertheless, the wrong man. The situation is further complicated by the fact that the right man has leprosy. However, the difficulties are resolved very simply. The husband is merely killed by lightning while on a picnic at Honk Falls. A doctor from Kingston develops a cure for leprosy. This cure, by the way, was found in Old 99's cave. It seems that Old 99 had leprosy and he developed a cure.

Apparently nothing stands in the way of the lovers being

united. Not so. Our hero feels duty bound to go to Hong Kong to work among the lepers there. However, as the book ends, and the setting sun casts long shadows across the Rondout Valley, his duty becomes clear. He must stay and marry the woman he loves.

At present, Miss Gray's book has become somewhat of a treasure. This last statement should be construed to mean that copies are difficult to obtain, not that it is a literary treasure. Its rareness must be ascribed to the fact that not too many copies were printed, and the literary tastes of the area have improved. This rareness has led to a complication in the legend of Old 99. Most people who have heard this legend recently, have heard it from sources that originally read the book. As a result, most people in the Warwarsing area relate the story of Benny Depuy and the Indian, Neopakintic, as previously told.

However, in the words of 88 year old, E. B. Ter Bush of Ellenville, "That damn book made a myth out of it'". Mr. Ter Bush remembers, ""the real story about Old 99's Cave", which he heard long before the book was written.

"In the first place", he says, "Old 99 was a Scotsman, not an Indian. This Scotsman, who was friendly with the Indians, was blindfolded and led up the mountain and into a cave, When the blindfold was removed, he found himself in a mine staring at a vein of pure silver." Mr. Ter Bush relates that after the Scotsman was blindfolded and led out of the cave again, he resolved to find that mine. He searched for it winter and summer for over seven years and finally found it. It was somewhere along what is now called the Mine Hole Brook, a swift mountain stream that cascades down the Shawangunks between the villages of Wawarsing and Kerhonkson. Mr. Ter Bush tells that the mountain was divided into lots in those days, and the cave was located on lot number 99. The Scotsman was so sure of the inaccessibility of the cave that he gave this much information about the mine's location when he came down with his silver. In time, the local residents came to call him "Old 99" and his real name has been lost to us.

He was a very enterprising man and he soon became dissatisfied with the business of selling ore. He decided to go into business that was more lucrative despite the fact that it was a tight monopoly. The government took an extremely dim view of Old 99's enterprise of minting U. S. silver dollars. He was arrested and put in jail in Kingston. His familiar figure, made more familiar by the prosperous jingle of shiny new silver dollars clinking in his pockets, disappeared from the local scene.

When Old 99, the Scotsman, was brought to trial, a most singular fact developed. This we know because the trial was attended by James Ter Bush, grandfather of E. B. Ter Bush, who related this tale. It seems that evidence was introduced in which it was shown that the coins minted by Old 99 contained more silver and hence were more valuable than the inferior product produced by the government. Common sense won the day, and the jury acquitted Old 99. In these days of the devalued dollar, this shining example of a practical solution to a perplexing problem must stand. Ulster should erect a statue to this primitive economist.

Alas, this was his moment of triumph. A dire fate was in store for him. He decided now to mine silver on a large scale. He needed help and he chose a partner, a man named Jacobus Bruyn. He blindfolded Mr. Bruyn and led him to the cave to show him the silver. Old 99 gathered a sizeable quantity, and after blindfolding his partner again, they came down off the mountain. Old 99 then notified Bruyn that he was going back to Scotland for a brief visit and that upon his return, he would show Bruyn the way to the cave. After that, they would be equal partners and work the mine together. Like his predecessors, Governor Wilhelmus Kieft, and his messenger Arend Corssen, Old:99 embarked with a treasure and like those two ill-fated adventurers, the ocean holds him and his secret ,for his ship foundered in the crossing. Jacobus Bruyn and the enterprising Ulstermen of the succeeding generations have since looked in vain for Old 99's cave.

Perhaps this version is a more authentic one than the one concerned with the Indian, Neopakintic. The fact that this legend continued to live in the Shawangunks is further evidenced by the writings of Arthur O. Friel. Mr. Friel wrote two books about the Shawangunks, ""Cat O'The Mountain", and "Hard Plrood", in the early nineteen twenties. "Hardwood", is a work of fiction but it is based on authentic legends and describes the actual Shawangunk locale. Mr. Friel describes what may be the last word in the legend of "Old 99's Cave", as follows:

"Now, three-four years back, there was a city feller into here awhile, name o' Hampton. He could lick his weight o' wild-cats, an' him an' me got to be pretty good friends. Wal, he was a-huntin' 'round quite a long spell for a feller that was a-hiding out from him, an' while he was a-hunting he found Ninety Nine's Mine. This Ninety-Nine's Mine had been lost a good many years - - ever since the Injuns died out - - an" a good many fellers had hunted for it without no luck. An' now Hampton, he found it, but he didn't want it. So he told me an' Uncle Eb we could have it an' make what we could outen it; an' then he went out, back to Noo York.

"Wal was a comins on winter then, so me an' Uncle Eb, we let it lay till spring. An' we talked about it a lot into the winter, an' Uncle Eb he used to say, "We'll find it awright - God willin'.' An' I'd say, "seein' Hampton put it all down onto paper, we'll find it anyways - - God willin' or not.' Uncle Eb he didn't like it, but I said it jest the same.

"Wal, come spring, we: couldn't find the paper. We knowed jest where 'twas put, but when we came to look for it, 'twasn't there no more. What'come of it, we dunno.

"But, I 'membered what was onto that paper, so I went an' hunted. An' I fell down and broke my arm. When that got well I hunted some more, an' some way I kep' a-gettin' hurt. But bimeby I found the place - - or what used to be the place. Everything was like Hampton said, 'ceptin' this: a piece o' rock bigger'n two houses had fell down right onto the little hole a-leadin' into the mine. It had fell down sometime into the winter while I was a-makin' fun o"God Willin". An' it jest kilt the onliest chance of ever gitten' into that mine.

"What's more, that rock warn't an overhang, li'ble to fall any time.'Twas a great big wedge o' straight -up-an' -down rock that got pried out - - someway - - from the side o' Dickie Barre to fall onto that one place. When I studied it all out I -wal, Hard, I got kind o' shivery. I ain't never been nigh the place sence. An' I don't made fun o"God Willin' 'no more."

His companion stared at him. Steve's quiet confession was impressive. Soon, however, a mirthless smile quirked Hard's mouth.

"A good stiff snort o' giant powder'd fix yer 'God-Willin'' 'rock, I bet."

The other tolerantly shook his head.

"Nope. It'd fetch 'bout a thousand ton more rock a' smashin' down. I thought o' that myself. The place is right 'tween two walls o" rock, an' one of'em is jest a-waitin' for some fool to shoot a blast into there. The man ain't a-livin' that'll ever get into that mine now. It's lost for good an' all."

Variations on the Theme /10

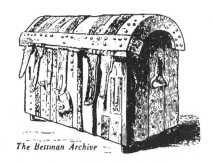

The Bettman Archive

    The " great wall" of the Shawangunks separates the Rond-out Valley from the Wallkill Valley. In days gone by, before the time of good roads and modern transportation, this great wall separated the peoples of these two valleys from one another. Crossing over was a very dangerous undertaking and only the hardiest dared brave the cliffs and crevasses on the poorly marked trail from Port Hixon on the west side and the village of Shawangunk on the east. On this trail, the notorious Indian, Shanks Ben murdered John and Elsie Mack during the Revolutionary War. This event further discouraged travel and communication between the two valleys.

    One of the results of this isolation is that the people of the Wallkill Valley on the east, knew nothing of the legend of Old 99's Cave. But there is a compensation. The people of the Rondout

Valley on the west, have never heard of Rufe Evans' Mine.

According to Johannes Upright of Rutsonville, who recently celebrated his 90th birthday, Rufe Evans was a good friend of the Indians. "Uncle Dick" Evans, Rufe's brother, was a very old man when Mr. Upright was a boy and it was "Uncle Dick" who told this story to Mr. Upright.

Rufe Evans was a very good friend of the few Indians who were left in the area at the time. He used to supply them with food and periodically they would appear with a bag of silver to pay him. He asked where they got the silver and the Indians refused to say more than, "In the mountains" In time, they agreed to show Rufe Evans where the mine was and, of course, they blindfolded him and led him up into the mountains. Apparently they were in no hurry to get back because they kept Rufe up there for several days. The mine was a spacious cavern and there were rich veins of silver ore in the walls. Finally, the Indians decided to return with Rufe. As they stepped out into the daylight, a slight accident occurred, the blindfold slipped down. Before the Indians could replace it, Rufe got a quick look at his surroundings and one landmark stood out. He was facing the steeple of the Shawangunk Church head on. Despite this slip, the Indians returned him safely but warned him not to try to find the mine. Rufe could see that they meant business and while the Indians remained in the area, he -was afraid to search for it. Years later, when the last Indian disappeared from the valley, Rufe Evans began his long search. Time had dimmed his memory and the changing seasons bad altered the face of the' mountain. Rufe Evans' mine was never found. It is still sought.

II

Another familiar tale of the Shawangunk treasure has a touch of the supernatural about it. It is sometimes referred to as "The Legend of the Candles". This story has many forms but is constant in one respect. A mysterious light or flame appears over the Shawangunks for a short period of time and then disappears. This mysterious flame is usually blue and it occurs over the mouth of a mine containing treasure. One of the witnesses, Mrs. David Townsend of Tillson Lake, reported that she saw it about 25 years ago in the area where Rufe Evans' mine is thought to be. "It was about 11 o'clock at night and I was alone in the house", Mrs. Townsend said, "~Then suddenly I saw this blue flame shoot out of the mountain. It went away up and died out and then another and another. In both directions, Flip! Flip!," she continued, throwing her arms over her head. "Now I'm not saying it was anything spooky", she said, " it was probably just gas coming out of a cave, but I wonder what lit it?"

III

An old story is related in a book called "Old Mine Road" written by C. S. Hine in 1908. This book describes the scenery and people encountered by Mr. Hine on a walking trip along this historic thoroughfare from Kingston to the Pahaquarry Mine Holes in New Jersey. He tells of a 12 year old boy who was befriended by an Indian chief. In time, as their friendship ripened, the Indian chief decided to take the boy into his confidence - - with reservations. The boy was blindfolded and the chief led him into the mountains. Then, after much walking and turning, he led the lad into a cave.

When the blindfold was removed, the lad saw a solid vein of silver. Mr. Hine says the lad was returned as he came, blindfolded, and no amount of searching could discover the treasure, but every seven years a bright light like a candle flame rises at 12 o'clock at night and disappears into the clouds. Many have seen the phenomenon and sought its source, but none have succeeded. The last time this was seen was in July, 1906, when according to New York papers, a "large ball of fire" hovered above Old Shawangunk several nights in succession. The latter part of this legend, dealing with the flame every seven years, was also described in the book "Old 99's Cave" and as a result, "The Legend of the Candles" has now become a part of the legend about Old 99's Cave. In connection with the legend just related, it is interesting to observe that it was an Indian chief who showed the boy where the treasure was. Perhaps Miss Gray, in writing her book thought that an Indian chief would make a more romantic "Old 99" than a Scotsman.

The Lost Gold Mine of the Hudson / 11

The river hills are a small range between the Shawangunk Mountains and the Hudson River. They separate the Wallkill Valley from the Hudson River Valley and gentle as they are, they formed in days gone by, a barrier between the peoples of these two valleys. Just as the people of the Wallkill knew nothing of Old 99's cave, the people on the far side of the river hills, knew nothing of Rufe Evans' mine, and of course, the peoples of the Rondout and Wallkill Valley, had never heard of the "Lost Gold Mine of the Hudson."

This story was set down in a slender volume by Tristam Coffin in 1915 in a hook that was published by Knickerbocker Press. An old hermit, by the name of Truman Hurd lived alone in a small but neat cabin just outside one of the Hudson River villages. He had settled there after the Revolutionary War and it was said that he had originally come from New England. Hurd, the old hermit, did not mingle with the village folk except when he had to come to town to buy provisions. He paid for these in gold coin. The only visitor that used to go to Hurd's cabin was the Esopus Indian, Uscung who used to come down from the Kingston area periodically and he would stay for several days at a time. Passersby noted that there would be lights in the cabin only on the evening of his arrival and on the evening of his departure. The cabin was apparently deserted on the other nights. In time, the people surmised that these two had a mine and a bold pair of villagers tried to follow them one evening. The Indian and the hermit, realizing they were being followed, hid in the bushes and sprang out at the two village folk, shrieking and brandishing weapons. The men fled in fear of their lives and in telling the story to the people back in the village, they embellished it to minimize their own cowardice. As a result, no one else ever tried to follow them again.

One day, the old hermit called the village doctor and told him that he wanted to make out a will. This doctor was the only man in the village that the old hermit would trust completely. In this will, he made the Indian, Uscung, one quarter beneficiary and he told the doctor that he owed all his wealth to this Indian. He also showed the doctor a hidden compartment in one of the rafters in the cabin where his wealth was kept. Shortly 1-hereafter, Hurd died and the doctor tried to locate Uscung. He learned that in the intervening time, Uscung too, had gone to his happy hunting ground. The doctor then went to the cabin and emptied the secret compartment. In it were thousands of gold coins, nuggets, and bank notes.

The estate was divided among several distant relatives of the old hermit.

The village people now realized that their suspicions about the secret mine were true and they realized further, that the only two people who knew about it, Uscung the Indian, and Truman Hurd the old hermit, were now dead. It was rumored that Hurd had saved the Indian during the war and this same Indian was the only survivor of his tribe who knew the location of the mine. It was reputed to be the same Indian mine that had excited the avarice of Henry Hudson's expedition which had mistakenly thought that this mine was located in the Shawangunks.

For a long period of time after the death of the old hermit, the villagers searched for it without success. One day, two 16 year old farm boys who lived on adjoining farms, outfitted themselves for this same search. Apparently they did not anticipate being away from home long but they did take the precaution of bringing two candle lanterns. As they were wandering it began to rain and they sought shelter at the base of a cliff. It rained violently all afternoon and now night was falling. They decided to spend the night there and as they sought shelter under the overhanging cliff, they noticed a deep cleft. They went into this cliff and followed a long and twisting passage which led into a huge cavern and when they stepped into this huge cavern, both candles could not illuminate it completely. They looked around and knew that they had found the old mine. They stumbled upon a primitive smelting plant, an iron and mortar pestle, a crucible, a small sledge hammer, steel drills and several bottles containing colored liquids. Around the floor were scattered charcoal and sticks of wood. A tattered blanket remained, as did an old work bench. Off in the distance they could hear water falling. The day's exertion and the excitement caused by their discovery, drained them of all energy and they curled up and went to sleep on the old blanket.

When they awoke they had no idea of what time it was. They lit their lanterns again and began to explore the cavern. They found veins of gold in the wall and stuffed their pockets with nuggets of gold and they found a few small refined bars of solid gold. They decided to leave in order to get a means of carting away more of the treasure. They turned to the passage by which they came and as they held the lantern high above their heads, they saw two bright coals glaring at them, the eyes of some beast of prey. They hurled several nuggets at it and the shrieks of the wounded beast told them it was a panther. In fear of their lives, they hurled nuggets at the beast and drove it growling down the passageway, but they were afraid to follow it for fear it might be lurking to spring upon them. They went back into the cavern and investigated the sound of the falling water that they had heard earlier. There they saw a spring and next to the spring was another passage. They followed this twisting passage further and further until they were almost sure it was a blind alley. Suddenly as they held the lantern up above their heads, they saw a thousand tiny bright lights. As they investigated further they saw that these were bats hanging from the ceiling and they knew there must be exit to the outside, nearby. They came to a very narrow opening, from which they could feel fresh air blowing, and their frantic hands tore away the stones and debris that were blocking this passage. A faint light coming from around a turn revealed that they had found another way out. When

64

they emerged they felt as if they were reborn. They looked around them and they were facing the Wallkill Valley. They realized that they had gone right through the river hills, entering on the east and emerging on the west. Nearby was a farm house and here they were fed. The farmer was leaving for their village and took them home by wagon, wondering all the time who these two tight-lipped boys were.

By the time their had returned, their parents had informed the community of their absence and whole parties of searchers were out looking for them. When the search was called off and the neighbors had left the boys told their parents of their discovery and they showed the remaining few nuggets that they had not thrown at the panther. The parents were elated and proud of their two courageous boys and like so many of the other seekers of treasure, they sat and spun the golden dreams that their wealth would bring them.

The weather got bad again and while the storm continued, they made plans for their expedition into the river hills to get the gold. Just before they started, there was a violent earthquake, one that was spoken of for long years in the Hudson Valley. The boys and their parents looked for the entrances to the cave on both sides of the hills but the cliffs had fallen and the entrances were never again found. In time, the boys learned to accept their disappointment and they settled down to lead normal lives. One married the sister of the other. The second boy married the daughter of the farmer whose house they first visited when they emerged from the mine and then, following the westward movement of the country, both families moved to the Finger Lake region where their descendants are now healthy and numerous.

Captain Kidd / 12

Mention buried treasure to most people and the word "pirate" comes to mind. Mention pirate and "Captain Kidd" the most famous of them all, comes to mind. At this point, the reader who feels that his credulity has been imposed upon will throw up his hands and say, "Now don't tell me Captain Kidd, the terror of the Spanish Main, had anything to do with the Catskills."

Hold your skepticism, for not only will you learn that this story provides a possible explanation of how treasures of a foreign culture came to reside in "Old 99's Cave", but you will also see at the end of this tale, how a good story about treasure is a source of treasure itself when whispered into the ears of gullible people.

Captain Kidd was baptized, William, when he was born in

the mid sixteen hundreds near Greenoch, Scotland, the son of an eccentric clergyman. Little is known of his early life before he went to sea. He first attracted public notice fighting heroically for the British against the French in 1688 during the dispute about the New World Colonies. Indeed in 1691, the British gave him a special award of 150 pounds for his outstanding services.

At one time, Captain Kidd made his home at the corner of Cedar & William Streets in New York City and there he took a wife. He came to the attention of Lord Bellomont of England who called for his services. 1695 found him in England where Lord Bellomont armed and outfitted the good ship, "Adventure Galley" for him. He received his commission from the King of England to fight pirates and to take reprisals against the French. He sailed with a crew of 80 men, for New York from Plymouth in April 1696. On the way over he captured a French ship. Upon arrival in New York, he remained for three or four months, recruiting volunteers. When he finally got his crew up to one hundred and fifty five men he set sail on a great voyage. This trip took him to Maderas and then to Vonavista and to St. Jago. From there he sailed to Madagascar, then to Calcutta, and back again to Madagascar. During this voyage he was still under the Kings commission and all of his plunder was "legal". He sailed from Madagascar for the West Indies and the famous Spanish Main. On this voyage he came upon the richly ladened Moorish ship, the Quedah Merchant and seized it intact. Captain Kidd then took 40 shares of the spoil and the rest was divided among his crew. Next he burned his own appropriately named ship, "Adventure Galley" and took command of the Quedah Merchant. Vlre can only surmise that the Moorish crew was forced to walk the plank.

Captain Kidd arrived at the Spanish Main without further incident and after spending a short time there, he set sail for Boston in a sloop ladened with his own share of the spoils. He left the Quedah Merchant under the command of his most trusted mate, Bolton. While Captain Kidd was sailing for Boston in August 1698, the East India Company informed the Lord Justices that Kidd had committed several acts of piracy on the high seas, citing the case of the Quedah Merchant specifically. He made several stops on his way to Boston burying his treasure. One of the stops he made was on Gardiner's Island on the Eastern end of Long Island. Here at a later date treasure valued at 14,000 pounds was found, a circumstance that has provided constant hope to all who sought elsewhere, in later times.

When Captain Kidd arrived in Boston he was recognized and arrested. He was sent to England in 1699, tried, found guilty, and hung by the neck until dead.

Bolton, who remained in command of the Quedah Merchant, heard about Captain Kidd's sad end and set sail for home. Most of his crew were New Yorkers and many of them, legend tells us, were from the Highlands of the Hudson. They planned to pass the Highlands, divide their booty, and then scuttle the Quedah Merchant. If they could accomplish this, they could then settle down to enjoy the life of plenty that their plunder would afford.

With this in mind, they silently sailed past New York City in the black of night and entered the Hudson. They continued on up the river and a storm overtook them just as they were entering the Highlands. Here at the foot of Dunderberg, the dreaded Thunder Mountain of the early Dutch navigators, the Hudson makes a sharp bend as it enters its most treacherous stretch, "The Race". There is a point of land at the foot of Dunderberg and here the Queda Merchant was scuttled because the crew feared to continue on in the storm. The crew, not taking time to divide it, took as much of the treasure as they could carry and hauled it away into the mountains where it was again hidden - - - - perhaps in Old Ninety Nine's Cave and there perhaps it still lies.

Some thought that the treasure was hidden near the "Duyvels DansKammer" the Devils Dance Chamber, an area on the west bank just above Newburgh where the Indians used to have their dances, pow-wows, and festivals. This was searched without success.

Others thought that it was hidden somewhere in a two mile long ridge on the west bank called Crow's Nest. There is a mass of rock projecting from the face of the cliff called, Kidd's Plug Cliff. This name was based on the story that the projection formed a plug to the cave in which Captain Kidd's treasure was hidden. How the pirates managed to put the plug in is not related.

About one hundred and twenty five years after Captain Kidd did his final jig, a river boat was anchored off Kidd's Point, as the projection at the foot of Dunderberg came to be known. The skipper called for the anchor to be raised and he found that it was fouled. It was raised by great effort and when it broke water, it was seen that it was snared on an old cannon. This was immediately proclaimed to be a gun from the Quedah Merchant, although some skeptics said it was from a British Man of War which was sunk during the Revolution. Then rumors were circulated that a long auger had been made and that it bored through the deck of the sunken ship. When the auger was brought to the surface, pieces of silver were caught in the thread.

A stock company was formed and over twenty thousand dollars was collected. A huge caisson or coffer-dam was built around the wreck. A powerful pump driven by a large steam engine was obtained to pump the area within the caisson dry. Then the funds ran low or more probably the promoters feeling that no more money would be raised, and knowing that no treasure could be raised, left with their swag donated by the gullible river folk.

The Captain Kidd legend had an interesting renaissance in November of 1869. In the grounds adjacent to the William Ellison house at New Windsor, below Newburgh, in November of 1869, Silas Corwin, the father of William Corwin, the owner at that time, was digging in the ground. His spade struck a hard object and he excavated around it. At first it looked like an old piece of Indian pottery but after digging around, he discovered it was intact. He reached down and pulled up an old jug of unknown origin. It seemed extremely heavy for earthenware. Mr. Corwin turned the jug upside down, expecting to see water run out of it and was astounded at the stream of silver coins. Six hundred and fifty pieces of eight spilled to the ground. The astounded man had really found buried treasure.

Word spread through the neighborhood like wild fire and further excavations were undertaken all around the house, all without avail. In speculating about the origin of these coins, the talk naturally turned to Captain Kidd's buried treasure. Here at last, said many of the local folk, is the vindication of the Captain Kidd legend, However, a local historian burst the bubble of these illusions when he pointed out that the pieces of eight were dated from 1621 to 1773, and by 1773 Captain Kidd had already become a legend.

The Bettman Archive

Giants in the Earth /13

"Roxbury, 10 July, 1706. Sir: - - I was surprised a few days since with a present laid before me from Albany by two honest Dutchmen, inhabitants of that city, which was a certain tooth accompanied with some other pieces of bone, which being but fragments, without any points whereby they might be determined to what animals they did belong, I could make nothing of them; but the tooth was of the perfect form of the eye tooth of a man, with four prongs or foots and six distinct faces or flats on the tops a little worn, and all perfectly smoothed with grinding. I suppose all the surgeons in town have seen it, and I am perfectly of opinion it was a human tooth. I measured it, and as it stood upright it was six inches high lacking one-eighth, and round 13 inches, lacking one-eighth, and its weight in the scale was 2 pounds, 3 ounces Troy weight. One of the same growth, but not of equal weight, was last year presented to my Lord Cornbury, and one of the same figure exactly was shown at Hartford of near a pound weight more than this.

Upon examination of the two Dutchmen they tell me the said tooth and bones were taken up under the bank of Hudson's river, some miles below the city of Albany, about 50 leagues from the sea, about - - - feet below the surface of the earth, in place where the freshet does not every year rake and waste the bank, and that there is a plain discoloration of the ground 75 feet at least, different from the earth in color and substance, which is judged by everbody that see it to be the ruins and dust of the body that bore these teeth and bones.

I am perfectly of opinion that the tooth will agree only to a human body, for whom the flood only could prepare a funeral; and without doubt he waded as long as he could to keep his head above the clouds, but must at length be confounded with all other creatures, and the new sediment after the flood gave him the depth we now find.

I remember to have read somewhere a tradition of the Jewish Rabbins, that the issues of those unequal matches between heaven and earth at the beginning were such whose heads reached the clouds, who are, therefore, called Nephelim, and their issue were Geborim, who shrank away to the Raphaim, who were then found not to be invincible, but fell before less men - - the sons of the east in several places besides Canaan. I am not perfectly satisfied of what rank of classis this fellow was, but I am sure not of the last, for Goliath was not half so many feet as this fellow was ells long.

The distance from the sea takes away all pretension of its being a whale or animal of the sea, as well as the figure of the tooth; nor can it be any remains of the elephant - - the shape of the tooth and measurement of the body in the ground will not allow that.

There is nothing left but to repair to those antique doctors for his origin, and to allow Dr. Burnet and Dr. Whiston to bury him at the Deluge, and if he were what he shows, he will be seen again at or after the conflagration further to be examined.

I am, sir, your humble servant,

J. DUDLEY"

So wrote his excellency, Hen. Joseph Dudley, Captain-General and Governor-in-Chief of Massachusetts Bay by appointment of her Majesty Queen Anne of England. The recipient of this scientific epistle was none other than Cotton Mather, fiery Pastor of the Second Church of Boston, prominent at that time as the most learned man in the colonies. He was the authority on all matters biblical and scientific and had recently distinguished himself by burning a goodly number of the citizens of Salem whom, by virtue of his extensive knowledge, he discovered were really witches.

Keeping this letter in mind, let us turn the spotlight of history ahead about 100 years and focus it down on the township of Rochester in Ulster County. Here one day, the son of Dan Bell, came upon a most extraordinary find at the bottom of a stream. It was a "giant" sword. This gargantuan weapon was almost six feet long and the wicked blade was fitted to a hilt designed to be grasped by two huge hands, hands strong enough to wield a seventeen pound sword. The hilt was inscribed with the script of a strange language, one which no one could read.

Were there then, giants in the earth in the Shawangunk area, sword-wielding giants? The answer, dear reader is yes - - with qualifications. The giants were of the tusk-wielding variety, not of the sword-wielding. Let us then dispose of the sword and get on to the tusks.

The father of the boy who found the sword was Dan Bell, a poor man, rich in inspiration. Dan was among the last of the breed called "pettifogers" and he had devised many schemes to get rich not only quickly, but more important, easily. At one time he mined gold in the Shawangunks. Another time he placed a boom across the Rondout Creek and filed a claim for all the gold washed down. In the words of the modern confidence man, Dan's latest "caper" began to look bad when the sword was taken down to New York City where it was examined by experts. They were too sharp to be taken by the sword and pronounced it a fake. The episode was covered by the New York papers and the notoriety helped Dan. He took the sword back home where he charged admission to see it. However, the "caper" collapsed a short time later when a sullen blacksmith appeared and demanded in public, to be paid for the giant sword that he had forged.

The skeleton which was the subject of Governor Dudley's letter marked the second of a long line of discoveries which were later identified as a new species of fossil elephant. This species was given the awesome title, Mastodon Giganteum Americanus, the Giant American Mastodon. During the Pleistocene period as the last glacier of the ice age began the retreat to its polar home, the Mastodons followed it north, till the herd found an ideal home.

Here were thousands of acres of swampy upland, covered with small trees, thickets, bushes and grasses on which they fed. To the west of their feeding ground loomed the Shawangunks, to the east the Hudson created a natural barrier. Here, in what is now Orange County, they thrived and multiplied. Then unaccountably, this race of giants became extinct. There were no men then who by merciless slaughter cut them down to the oblivion of extinction, the fate that befell the clouds of passenger pigeons that later darkened Catskill skies.

The ice did not return nor is there evidence of any other natural cataclysm. Of the more than 30 skeletons that have been found in this area, almost all have been in an upright position bogged down in the peat and mart of prehistoric swamps. In the rib cages there was the finely chewed twigs and vegetation, the last meal taken at the swamps edge. Yet it is unlikely that one by one, seeking the more tender shoots on softer ground, they ate their way to extinction. Rather, we are faced with the deepest designs of nature, that creates species, races and nations, gives them sway and then grinds them back to the dust of the ages. In 1846, Samuel Eager, Orange County Historian, speculated upon the fate of the Mastodon:

"Upon these subjects, wrapt in the deep mystery of many ages, we have no fixed or well-considered theory; and if we had, the limits of our paper would forbid us to argue it up before our readers, and argue down all hostile ones. But we may briefly enquire, whether the cause of the death and utter annihilation of the race, was one great overwhelming flood which submerged the earth and swept down these animals as they peacefully and unsuspiciously wandered over the plains and hills around us. Or was it some earthquake convulsion, full of sudden wrath, which tore up its strong foundations and buried this race among the uplifted and subsiding mass of ruins; or was it some unusual storm, black with fury and terrible as the tornado, which swept the wide borders of these grounds, and carried tree and rock and living Mastodon in one unbroken stream to a common grave? Or was it the common fate of nations, men and every race of created animals of water, land, or air, which overtook and laid the giants low? that by the physical law of their nature, the decree of heaven, the race started into being - - grew up to physical perfection - - and having fulfilled the purpose assigned by their creation, by a decrease slow, but sure as their increase, degenerated in number, and gradually died away and became extinct. Or was it some malignant distemper, fatal as the Egyptian murrain, which attacked the herd in every locality of this wide domain - - sending its burning poison to their very vitals - - forcing them to allay an insatiate thirst and seek relief in the water ponds around them, and there drank, and drank, and died? Or was it rather, as is the general belief in this community, that individual accident, numerous as the race, befell each one, and in the threes of extrication sank deep and deeper still in the soft and miry beds where we now find their bones reposing?"

The bones of this Elephants' Graveyard east of the Shawangunks grace the museums of the world. The first Orange County skeleton was exhumed near the village of Montgomery, and General Washington who was encamped at nearby Newburgh in 1182 came to examine the bones. Some of these found their way to Germany thanks to the Physician General of the Hessian troops and others ended up in a Philadelphia museum.

Around 1800 a number of other finds were made in the area, from which the elephant-like nature of the animal was determined. A fine specimen was discovered in the adjoining town of Shawangunk in Ulster County. This find came to the attention of a great naturalist who, at the time, happened to be Vice-President of the United States. His name was Thomas Jefferson. Within a month he became President. In an article called, "Jefferson as a Naturalist", an earlier writer comments, "Thus, during those exciting weeks in February, 1801, when Congress was vainly trying to untangle the difficulties arising from the tie vote between Jefferson and Burr, when every politician in the capital was busy with schemes and counterschemes, this man, whose political fate was balanced on a razor's edge, was corresponding with Dr. Wisner in regard to some bones of the mammoth which he had just procured from Shawangunk, Ulster County."

Jefferson obtained both the upper and lower jaws of the Shawangunk Mastodon, and eventually presented them to the University of Virginia.

Each of the discoveries of Mastodon remains were sought for eagerly by scientists. No complete skeleton had been found, although composite skeletons had been put together. This led to competition by the scientists from the various institutions to be first on the scene to claim or purchase the bones. In the case of the Mt. Hope skeleton, found at the Mitchell farm on the Shawangunk Mountain in 1812, Professor Waterhouse Hawkins of Princeton was racing Professor O. C. Marsh of Yale to the scene. Fate placed them on the same train to nearby Otisville, unknown to one another. At the point nearest the Mitchell farm, the train slowed down almost to a stop and a gentleman swung down. It was Professor Marsh of Yale. Hours later when Professor Hawkins arrived, he was greeted by Professor Marsh who informed him that the Mastodon decided to go to Yale. The Marsh skeleton, as it came to be called, was complete except for a few bones in the hind legs. When it was assembled, it was 10 feet high, 15 feet long, and weighed over 1700 lbs.

The conductor was later asked by a friend why he slowed at an unscheduled place to let Professor Marsh off the train. The conductor replied, flicking an ash off his fine Havana Cigar, C' You see, that fellow had some really good cigars with him."

The preceding stories in this book have dealt with events in the early days of our country. The Revolutionary War seems incredibly remote and the days when the Dutch came here and overran the Indians have in themselves the hazy outline of Legend. Yet these spans of time are a fleeting instant in the story of life and who among us can visualize or recreate the days when the valleys in the shadows of the Shawangunks trembled under the pounding footfall of the Mastodon?

The Salt of the Earth /14

The salt of the earth. Here is a term that has two meanings. First it describes the simple common folk who were victims of this tale, and secondly it describes the means by which they were victimized.

Shortly after the Civil War, a man by the name of Eli Wilkinson came from the west and settled in Rutsonville, a tiny hamlet along the eastern base of the Shawangunks. He bearded with two old time residents, Mr. and Mrs. Lockwood, who apparently needed the extra income because they had 11 daughters to support.

Often in the long winter evenings, Mr. Wilkinson would captivate the Lockwood family with tales of his youth. He had prospected for gold and had participated in the gold rush of '49 in California. Presently he confided that it was the quest for gold that brought him into the Shawangunks. This, he explained, was the reason for his long hikes and frequent disappearances. During this period he singled out the eldest daughter, Eunice Lockwood, as the treasure dearest to his heart. Her feelings were the same and soon they married.

One day Eli returned from a prospecting trip full of elation. He had found some ore which looked promising. A small stamp mill was made, the ore was crushed and assayed. It was found to contain gold in promising quantities. Further samples were assayed and enough gold was refined to make a pair of earrings and a breast pin.

Eli Wilkinson convinced several members of the community that at last the Shawangunks would yield its treasure. A company was formed. Stock was issued. Mining was commenced. Under Hamilton Point and in view of Gertrude's Nose, two well-known landmarks, a shaft was begun. A small railway trestle was constructed so that the diggings could be carried out of the shaft on small cars. All this activity meant that the bubble was growing, according to Mr. P. E. Clark, at this writing in his 80's. Mr. Clark's uncle was an investor in the mine to the extent of $500. This uncle was one of Ellenville's most illustrious citizens, Dr. Scoresby, whose mansion is now the old wing of the Ellenville hospital, and in whose name Scoresby Hose does honorable battle to the flames that periodically threaten the community.

If such a pillar as Dr. Scoresby was toppled, what chance had the prudence of the common folk? Yes, when all the money had been collected and the stock issued, Eli Wilkinson "lit out" for the west with his bride and his money, both treasures of the Shawangunks. There he prospered, rose to be manager of the Golden Gate Hotel in San Francisco where he died at 106 after a life of adventure climaxed by the great earthquake of 1906 which he survived.

This is a true story and most of the details were given by Mr. Everett Aumick who has a farm in Rutsonville. Mr. Aumick's mother was Julia Lockwood, a sister of Eunice Lockwood Wilkinson. The gold earrings and the breast pin made from the ore Eli Wilkinson submitted are still in existence the property of Mrs. Charlotte Sempke of N. Y. C., daughter of Mr. Aumick and grand-niece of Eli and Julia Wilkinson. Mr. Aumick is convinced that gold was actually discovered, but in non-paying quantities. Just as certain are the children and grandchildren of the unfortunate investors. They are convinced that the mine was salted.

An interesting sidelight to this tale is a field trip which I made in an attempt to gather more definite material. One of Mr. Aumick's neighbors is Mr. Joe Skepmose, age 70, tall and straight as a ramrod. He is a man who was hewn from seasoned timber and in him one sees the breed that wrested the area from the Indians, the bears and the panthers. Joe was born in the shadows of these mountains, walked over every foot of the eastern side, and knows them like no living man today. It is a profound thing when a man as reticent and uncommunicative as he is, looks at the Shawangunks, turns and looks you straight in the eye saying, "Boy, I love those mountains". And love them he does. Not jealously either, for when I explained that my visit was to gather information about the Old Wilkinson mine he agreed to show me where it was.

On May 30, 1951, Memorial Day, Joe Skepmose and I set off from Rutsonville to visit the mine. Although he had not been there in over 20 years he had no hesitancy in blazing his trail up the slopes and along the cliffs. More amazing still was the vitality and sprightliness of this 70 year old. He leaped across streams, strode over fallen logs and clambered up ledges, hampered only by a man in his twenties who was struggling unsuccessfully to keep up with him.

We came at last to the old mine. The shaft was completely filled in. The crevice leading to the shaft had been dug long years ago. It was still covered with the diggings that had been removed from the shaft and nothing grows in it. All evidence of the trestle is gone but Joe still recalls the ruins of it. It is quite evident that there once was a mine here.

Then Joe told me of another place about a quarter of a mile along the mountain. This he called the Old Mine and told me that his father had referred to it by this name as had his father before him. No one recalled what was mined there.

Joe led me to it. It is located in a small canyon called Wolf's Jaw. There near a spring from which Joe drank on huckleberry picking excursions as a boy, was the Old Mine. There is water in the shaft and the entrance is strewn with rocks and boulders hacked from the shaft.

As we left, I asked "Joe, what do you think about these stories of gold?"

He answered, "I think there is gold in these mountains. I'd like to blast the entire side out between the Old Mine and Eli Wilkinson's Mine."

The Fountain of Youth /15

The Bettman Archive

Of all the treasures that man has sought through all time, there is one which has always eluded him. All avenues of approach have been attempted. All have failed. Some men have roamed the face of the earth for it. Others have made a compact with the devil and sold their souls for it and in recent times, the witch doctors of science have tried to achieve it with the surgeon's knife, but none has found the secret of eternal youth.

There is in the village of Ellenville, located in the Rondout Valley at the foot of the Shawangunk Mountains, a mysterious tunnel and an amazing spring. This tunnel is 6 feet high and 4 feet wide and goes straight into the bowels of the mountain for 515 feet, hacked through Shawangunk grit, one of the hardest types of rock known. At the end of this tunnel is a spring from which gushes at the rate of 30 gallons per minute, the purest water known to man.

Who dug this tunnel?

When was it done?

What was the nationality of the people who dug it?

By whose orders and authority?

What became of the people?

Why was it dug?

Not one of these questions can be answered! No mention is made of this tunnel in any historical document and its existence was unknown for an undetermined period of time, until it was rediscovered in 1905. There is a local legend explaining its origin.

This tradition relates that in the 1500's the greatest of all seekers of the Fountain of Youth, Pence de Leon, set forth for Florida in the great quest which eventually cost him his life. The legend relates that the group split and part of them went north continuing the search. In time they came to the foot of this mountain and beheld water of unusual sparkling purity gushing from a crevice in the mountain. They determined to find its source - - perhaps at last the long sought Fountain of Youth.

Straight back they hacked and chipped and drilled. They had no modern hardened steel or blasting powder. Tool marks on the wall and roof of the tunnel show primitive methods and puny tools were employed. Straight back they went, except once, when they followed some false lead to the right for 30 or 40 feet.

It must have taken many many months - - even years. Suddenly the tunnel ends. Why? Was it hostile Indians? Plague? Discouragement? Lack of Provisions? No one knows.

There are shafts into lead mines within a mile. These shafts are not nearly as long and are mentioned in many old maps and records going back to the 1600's and they produced lead up until this century. But there is no record or mention of the Old Spanish Tunnel. It is well known that there were Spanish people in the area from the earliest days. Indeed, the most spectacular scenic spot in the entire Shawangunk range is Sam's Point, named after the famous frontiersman of Spanish descent, Sam Gonsalus, who lived during the middle 1700's. Sam's Point bears his name because he jumped from that precipice into the top of a hemlock tree below to elude capture from a group of hostile Indians who thought they had at last cornered one of their most dangerous enemies.

There is another story that might be related to this old tunnel that goes back to the canal building days of the 1820's. According to an old story, a group of canal workers found an old cave, which according to descriptions, must have been in the vicinity of this old Spanish tunnel. The canal workers were convinced that great treasure lay further in the mountain and they began to fill the entire tunnel with blasting powder. They were planning to ignite this tremendous charge which probably would have blown half the side off the mountain and obliterated the village of Ellenville. However, their plan was discovered and halted.

Since 1905 many facts are available about the Old Spanish Tunnel. One of the first printed articles calling the tunnel by this name is the pamphlet printed by the Huntoon Spring Water Company, prior to 1910. In 1907, this company acquired property to the land upon which the tunnel and spring are located, and set up the Sun Ray Bottling Plant. This three story building was the largest bottling plant in the world. A host of independent chemists, bacteriologists and geologists were hired to test the water and it was their unanimous opinion that this was the purest natural water ever discovered.

The fame of the tunnel spread and in time, the curious came and were accommodated by a small railway which took sightseers through the tunnel, now illuminated by electric lights, back to the spring. The little cars which ran on the steel rails were pushed by guides. At the spring, the tourists would have a drink and perhaps toss a coin for good luck into the crystalline pool beyond the waist high dam that the Huntoon Spring Water Company erected.

During this period, the entrance to the tunnel was graced by a Roman archway with pillared supports and the area around the entrance was beautifully landscaped with formal gardens.

The origin of the tunnel was as much a mystery at that time as it is now, as proven by the following paragraph which appeared in the Sun Ray pamphlet:

"REWARD

One thousand dollars will be paid to the first person who can establish, beyond any doubt, the origin of the legends pertaining to, and the approximate construction of, the mysterious tunnel referred to on pages 1 to 3, from the farther end of which flows the famous Sun Ray Spring.

To this end, students of geology and archaeology and others interested in the above offer who desire to make investigation, are cordially invited to visit Ellenville, a charming village, located on the New York, Ontario and Western Railway, three hours ride from New York City, where every facility will be afforded for study and research. The trip in itself is a delightful outing."

The property changed hands several times during later years. Local people insist that the tourist trade to the springs was so brisk that the Saratoga Springs people bought it, under a different name, and closed it as a threat to their large investment upstate. The bottling plant and the water from the spring were used by a succession of soft drink manufactures. Later it was used by a cosmetic factory and at present it is a government warehouse.

Although the bottling plant has been used through the years, the last time that the tunnel was used was during the prohibition era of the 1920's. A gang of bootleggers, reputedly part of the Dutch Shultz syndicate, used the tunnel to hide illegal beer. There are still many kegs of old beer lying in the Old Spanish Tunnel and now, the smell is such that if Benny Depuy had been led in there blindfolded, he'd have sworn that he was being conducted through a brewery.

If only Pence de Leon again walked the earth continuing his search! He would come again to this tunnel and enter it. He would pause halfway down the tunnel and tap a keg of beer. (The author will testify that no lasting harm comes of this.) In time, as the contents of the keg were lowered, Pence would indeed recapture his lost youth. He would then proceed to the end of the tunnel, and looking with heavy eyes through the clear shimmering spring at the coins tossed in by bygone tourists, he would fancy that he saw pieces of eight dancing beneath the surface. And for a brief moment, he would rest his search for he had found at last that for which he had roamed the earth - - youth and wealth. If he were as much a philosopher as an adventurer, he would then realize that happiness is a condition of the mind, not a place reached or a thing achieved.

Hussey Hill Gold /16

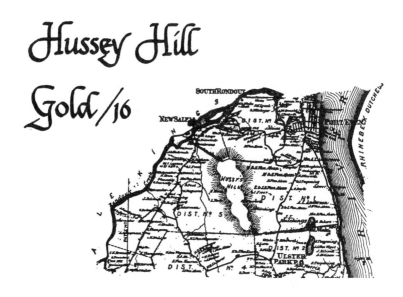

Hussey Hill is located just across the Rondout Creek from Kingston. From its summit most of the city can be seen. According to an ancient deed, it was named after Frederick Hussey who once owned the land in that area. No doubt this latter bit of information is a disappointment to those people to whom the word, L'Hussey" means a worthless woman and who therefore hoped to find a gayer story than that which follows. Actually, in this latter sense Hussey Hill is appropriately named, for as we shall see, it is a story of a worthless hill.

Our story goes back to April 1880 when the following appeared in the Rondout Freeman.

"Hussey Hill Gold"

"Mr. Floyd McKinstry was in town yesterday, and has now gone to New York accompanied by a barrel of Hussey Hill gold-

89

mine stone. Mr. McKinstry said yesterday, 'I have heard a vast amount of talk about Hussey Hill gold, and I am determined to see what there is in the stuff. So I have obtained some very fair samples of the rock quarried from the mine, and I am going to have it assayed. And what's more', continued the man from Gardiner, 'I am going to keep that barrel of rock under my eye all the way through. They won't have the chance to salt it. This is a square deal, and I am determined to see that the assay is made on the square. This will settle whether there is any bottom to this Ulster gold business.'

"The 'gold-rock' taken by Mr. McKinstry was taken up promiscuously from a pile containing upwards of two hundred tons that has been quarried from Hussey Hill. It was not 'picked', but taken up hit-and-miss, without regard to appearance. Mr. Louis I. Patchin, who is not interested in the mine, and who does not expect to be, vouched for this fact, and he joins with Mr. McKinstry in averring that this is a 'fair deal.' Much interest is felt in certain quarters as to the probable result of the assay which Mr. McKinstry will have made."

Not long after, this follow up story appeared in the same paper.

"Investigating Hussey Hill"

"A. R. Phyfe, the refiner who made the assay of Hussey Hill gold rock, and Thomas Binns, the inventor of the process under which the assay was made, were in town to-day, and accompanied John C. Brodhead and Simon S. Westbrook across the creek to Hussey Hill. It is said that an examination of the mine convinces them that there does exist gold at that point in paying quantities, and it is further declared probable that the result of their visit will be the enlistment of New York capitalists in the enterprise of energetically working this mine at an early date."

N. B. Sylvester in his "History of Ulster County" (1880) goes on to comment:

"These two items from the Freeman relate to an enterprise which is in the hands of men of judgment and superior business capacity. The mine alluded to is at the north end of Hussey Hill, town of Esopus, about three-fourths of a mile from South Rondout.

Samples of the rock have been submitted for assay to the following responsible authorities: John A. Waters' Sons, No. 11 John Street, New York; William C. Waters, No. 9 John Street; Fife & Waters, No. 17 John Street; William H. Dedrick, 21 William Street; Walter Hamilton, 120 William Street; Pier & Roberts, Brooklyn; Walker & Brothers, Philadelphia. The average result of all these assayers yields thirty-four dollars gold and silver from a ton of crude rock as taken from the mines. Small veins have been opened, yielding as high as five hundred and twenty-two dollars to the ton, under the tests of Messrs. Fife & Waters. So much confidence in this enterprise have the men who are in charge of it that they have erected a five-stamp mill, to be run by steam power, and have three thousand tons of rock upon the "dumps" ready for working. The vein to be worked is so exposed and so easy of access that one hundred tons of rock may be got out daily. The property is now in charge of Simon S. Westbrook and John C. Brodhead, who are now making arrangements to organize a company with capital sufficient to thoroughly test the feasibility of gold-mining in Ulster County."

After writing the above, Mr. Sylvester's book went to press

and he was spared the details of the sequel to this golden start. And perhaps unwittingly his words quoted above helped to swell the worth of the "worthless hill."

Another writer who mentions this subject William C. De Witt stated although the particles of ore were dull and dark the stock certificates which were sold were brilliant with gold letters. A persuasive sales agent circulated among the crowds that gathered on weekends, to observe the "diggings". According to De Witt, his best single sale came to $35,000 and his total sales were in excess of $150,000. The situation was similar to the one in an insane asylum where one of the inmates sat with a fishing pole in front of a bucket of water. A "normal" visitor from the outside stopped by and asked the inmate, "Have you caught anything yet?" "You're the fourth today," was the reply.

And so as in the case of Eli Wilkinson the denouement depends on whether the story comes to us from the descendants of the fisherman or of the fish.

Those of the fisherman say, "There was gold but not in paying quantities."

Those of the fish say, "We were robbed. The mine was salted."

There is Gold and Silver Too /17

The
OLD
MINE
ROAD

MINE
1906

Is there really gold or silver in the Shawangunks and the Catskills? Are these stories and legends just wishful fantasies devised by old men for the amusement of their grandchildren? Or is it possible that there is some definite geological evidence that these precious metals do exist? Undoubtedly these questions occurred to the more curious reader as he read these legends hopefully, only to share the final disappointment that seems to plague all seekers of treasure in these mountains.

These same questions constantly intruded as this book took form. As each of these stories was tracked down, I shared the hopes that kindled each project and then felt the same bitter disappointment when it didn't "pan-out". Finally "pay dirt"'. I uncovered proof that gold and silver definitely exists in the Shawangunks. My prospecting was not done with pick and shovel but by digging in libraries and by following up other leads.

The proof concerning silver was dug out of an official publication and of the two reliable accounts of gold the second has the familiar outline of the earlier legends; but since it is a true story the similarity now lends credence to the early accounts.

We can assure ourselves of the existence of silver by reference to our official New York State publication printed in 1950 entitled, "The Mineral Industries of New York State". On Page 46 there is a section with the Shawangunk Mountain area which states:

"The reports which deal with the zinc and lead ores of Shawangunk Mountains make no estimate of the ore reserves. Their present primary limitation lies in the mode of occurrence of the ore. The largest ore bodies are veins along the bedding planes, and these veins vary from a fraction of an inch to five feet in thickness. The individual veins pinch out at short distances. In the fissures that cross the bedding planes, ore has also accumulated, but these veins are rarely more than six inches wide and only a few feet in length. Finally, there are minor disseminations of ore, just bits here and there. The short individual veins and bits of ore are separated from each other by intervening masses of waste rock. In the 19th century, these small individual veins were exploited mainly with pick and shovel. Today, however, these hard methods cannot compete with large scale mechanized mining, and so modern mining technique is not economical where ores are so scattered and occur under such varied conditions. With modern methods, great masses of country rock would have to be moved for every ton of ore mined.

Despite these apparent limitations, the Shawangunk Mountain area should be kept in mind. It is possible that closer study may reveal additional ore deposits of economic dimensions and quality. During 1948 and 1949, the U. S. Bureau of Mines carried on an extensive program of diamond drilling at the long idle Summitville Mine near Wurtsboro. The results indicate a deposit of considerable extent which appears to maintain more uniform dimensions than any other deposit in the area. Analyses of Summitville ore have shown zinc values as high as 20.1 percent, with 12.9 percent of lead, 2.25 ounces of silver to the ton and undetermined amounts of copper."

Let us withhold comment on this description of the occurrences of the ore bodies and this conclusive reference to silver until we satisfy ourselves that also, "there is gold in them thar hills" Some of the stories collected in this book represent a great deal of leg-work and others many hours of research. However, our first account of gold actually was a "lucky strike". I had the good fortune to acquire a copy of the wonderful but rare book, "The Old Mine Road" by C. G. Hine, printed in 1909. Upon opening it an old clipping fluttered out. I picked it off the floor and was met by this headline. "3 Digging 'Gold' in Hills of Own Upstate Farm" The sub-head stated, "'Finchville farmer and two sons re-open 1785 shaft 75 miles from Broadway". The clipping which was from the New York Herald Tribune dated October 27, 1938 went on to state: "Middletown, N. Y.; October 21 - - Acting on the advice of E. Maltby Shipp, mining engineer of Newburgh and New York, fifty one year old David Hosking, Finchville farmer, has reopened a Colonial gold mine on his property, and today he revealed that preliminary assays have been sufficiently encouraging to warrant further prospecting.

Hosking, aided by his two sons, David and Lester, is digging his test shaft only a few feet from the entrance of an old and abandoned shaft believed to have been sunk at least 150 years ago. The farmer, whose land is on the summit of the Shawangunks, only seventy-five miles from New York City, knew that the older shaft had been opened in the expectation of finding gold and that some of the precious metal had been extracted.

The present prospectors' first task was to pump the old mine dry of water, which filled it nearly to the top and which may have been the reason that the shaft was deserted in an earlier age, which was not equipped to cope with such drainage problems. The water supply there was so constant that the Hosking family previously had it piped to their farmhouse.

At the bottom of the old shaft the diggers came upon some rust scarred drills and sledges, evidently used by the earlier fortune hunters. Keeping in constant touch with Mr. Shipp, who told him recently that one of the assays was even better than those made public, Hosking and his sons kept digging. The mine's yield thus far, however, has not been sufficiently good to warrant it on a commercial basis, according to Mr. Shipp's advice, and so the Hoskings dig only in the time they can spare from farming.

Hosking, whose father was once superintendent of gold and silver mines in Colorado, is not counting his chickens before they are hatched and said today, dryly: 'Well, I'm fifty-one years old, and I've never had any money, and I wouldn't mind having a little in my old age, but even if I don't get the gold I've still got the farm.' Hosking inherited the 145 acre farm from his father, who bought it when a mining concern had a ninety-nine year lease on it. The lease now has expired.

Gold has long been sought in the Shawangunks. Early Dutch adventurers searched for the ore on a long trip from Esopus (now Kingston) up the Rondout and down the Basha Kill, Neversink and Delaware Valleys, all the way to Pahaquarry Flats, near Delaware Water Gap. There, in the middle of the seventeenth century, they found copper and built what was then the longest road in this country back to Esopus, over which they transported the metal.

Quick reference to the map showed that Finchville is a tiny community on the east side of the Shawangunks just south of Otisville. The visit to the Hosking farm which followed was made exciting by two events. First I got to see Mr. Hosking's mine and secondly I was bitten by Mr. Hosking's dog. Let no one tell you that writing is not a hazardous occupation.

The mine entrance is still open. It is located under upturned outcropping of rock which forms a ledge. The ledge is unusual in that the planes of stone are at a 45 degree angle down and away from the face of the ledge. The mine shaft follows this stratification and goes into the ledge and down at the same time following the strata.

The light of the day reveals that, thirty feet from the entrance, the shaft is full of water. The sloping submerged shaft continues over 150 feet down ending in the watery blackness of an ocean trench. The mine is once again abandoned. The diggings almost block the entrance and in a few more years, wild foliage will finally seal it· There is gold in that mine. Other minerals too, but the most favorable assay shows only $3.50 per ton gold, $.50 per ton of silver and similar concentrations of lead and zinc. Pay dirt, yes. But not enough pay for the amount of dirt.

Our second reliable account of gold is a legend nipped in the bud. It is relatively recent and was circulated by word of mouth in the Ellenville area. When I first heard it, it seemed so familiar that I thought it was another version of Old Ninety Nine's Cave dressed in modern garb. There were four men concerned, but only one was identified by name. That man is a professional geologist. His name is Paul Bird and at this writing, he is employed by the New York State Department of Soil Mechanics. At the time that these events occurred he was employed as assistant geologist by the New York City Board of Water Supply. The Board of Water Supply was engaged in the gigantic task of building Merriman Dam on the Rondout Creek. This dam created the Rondout Reservoir in the Lackawack Valley, obliterating the old communities of Lackawack, Montela, and Eureka. Water from the reservoir is fed through a deep, tremendous tunnel which goes right under the Shawangunks to the east side where it joins the aqueduct running to New York.

While that tunnel was being dug there was an explosion deep under the mountains and eight tunnel workers were severely burned. They had hit a pocket of gas under high pressure. It was unexpected and unprecedented. The chief engineer called for Paul Bird and asked if it were possible to predict the recurrence of such gas pockets. Mr. Bird said that he did not know. The Chief Engineer then gave Mr. Bird the assignment of learning all that was possible to know of the geology of the Shawangunks. So for many months Paul Bird was a virtual ambassador without portfolio, going and coming as he pleased, learning more about the mountains than any native son.

One day in the summer of 1938 while he was on this assignment, two engineers who also worked for the Board of Water Supply called Paul Bird aside. They knew of his assignment and sought him out because they were in need of advice. Here was their quandry.

They had a mine on the mountain. It was being worked by a local man and the two engineers were putting up the money. They had several thousand dollars invested. The pump that they had bought was no longer adequate to cope with the increasing volume of water as the mine got deeper. And a new pump would cost $3000.00. Should they put up the additional money or abandon the mine?

They showed Paul an assay sheet prepared by the Ledoux Company in New York City and he was amazed to see that the sample assayed would yield $125.00 per ton. Paul said, "These figures show that it might well pay to expand operations. However, I can't definitely say without seeing the mine."

In the legends a blindfold is applied at this point. In this account, the universal blindfold, dark of night, was employed. Paul continued, "One night they took me by car along Route 209 to Fordmoore Road between Kerhonkson and Wawarsing. We went along Fordmoore Road to where it crosses Mine Hole Brook; Then we got out and walked. One fellow went ahead with a flashlight and he sure led us a merry chase. I think we circled around for about an hour until we came to the shaft. It was located at the foot of a cliff,"

They showed Paul the vein they were working. It was a minor fault about six inches wide and filled with clay. In the clay were crystals of iron pyrites, fool's gold. However, these men knew what fool's gold was and explained to Paul that there were small quantities of real gold in the pyrite crystals. When Paul questioned them further about the sample they had assayed it turned out that they had sent only iron pyrite crystals and in one ton of iron pyrite crystals there was $125 worth of gold or somewhat less than 3 ounces. Paul studied the structure of the seam and took a sample of the clay. His analysis showed that iron pyrites comprised only one percent of the clay vein. This meant that 100 tons of clay would have to be mined to get one ton of iron pyrites. This in turn would yield about 3 ounces of gold. To further dampen the project, he pointed out that the narrowest practical vein that could be mined was 3 feet. This meant that for every six inches of clay mined 21/2 feet of stone would be mined and Paul saw no reason to expect that further digging would reveal that the vein might widen.

And so, under Paul Bird's investigation, the $125 ton yield evaporated to an insignificant amount. The mine was closed and the project abandoned. Yet Paul says, "Gold is definitely present in small quantities. Wherever small quantities exist there is always the possibility of higher concentrations. In geology the unexpected is not too unusual. No one could have predicted the gas pockets we ran into. Yet there they were. The Shawangunks have not yielded all their secrets."

Let these words give heart to those who still seek treasure in our mountains.

The Blue Gold of the Catskills/18

Blue Stone Docks at Rondout

"Indeed to do more in an article, limited as this must be, is impossible, but had one the time, space and ability to tell them, there are stories as dramatic, thrilling and full of human interest to be told of this apparently dull subject as any ever told of the gold fields of California, the Black Hills or the Klondike, stories of wealth rapidly and unexpectedly acquired and often as rapidly lost, of joy and despair, of success and disappointment, of hope long deferred only to finally change to despair. For a bluestone quarry is a lottery and the quarryman who spends his time and money in removing tons of loose stone and earth from a promising looking block may win a prize or draw a blank - - he may win a succession of prizes or draw a succession of blanks, or, and this is even more disappointing, he may accumulate wealth by a long series of successful discoveries of excellent blocks and then lose all in unearthing a succession of worthless heaps of brittle stone. The last named experience has fallen the lot of many. Indeed the curse of the bluestone business has been that so few know when to stop - - so few have been able, when business began to be done at a loss instead of the former profit to resist the temptation to lose still more in the hope of ultimately winning back all the losses and a handsome profit besides. The desire, when loss begins, not to quit until it is at least retrieved, the extreme means resorted to attain this end, the completeness of the ruin following the final failure, are those common in all attempts at money making in which the element of chance enters, and no gambler at Monte Carlo, or one speculating in Wall Street, depends more upon chance than does the bluestone quarryman sweating and toiling in the foothills of the Catskills, sustained by the hope that the stone he has not yet seen may prove of value sufficient at least to repay him for his expenditures. Strange that the same gamblers' fever which throbs in the veins of the loser at the gaming table in the gilded gambling room should be akin to the force that animates the quarryman in some secluded spot in the hills strange but none the less true", so wrote De Lisser, in 1896 in his book, " Picturesque Ulster".

Stranger still and also true is the fact this Blue Gold supported thousands of men in the Catskill area, in an industry richer even than the fabulous cement and brick industries. The mountains were pock marked with hundreds of quarries. Roads and trails teemed with wagons and sledges dragging and tugging massive loads down to the docks. The docks were in turn, hives of tremendous activity where amid clouds of steam, derricks unloaded the stone into piles that stretched along the waterfront as far as the eye could see. Nearby in the clanging stone mills, tremendous slabs of bluestone, bolted to heavy timber carriages, oscillated back and forth, under huge planing knives. Next to these shrieking planers, on massive gang saws, some using diamond teeth, as many as six saw blades simultaneously, chewed through long slabs of "rock". And neighbor to these grit covered contraptions, on wildly rotating rubbing machines, great circular cast iron plates smoothed the bluestone surfaces by grinding them under a constant jet of sand and water. Alongside these feverish mills, gangs of men toiled with muscle and derrick to load the finished products into the holds of empty barges which were waiting to transport the stone to the great American cities that were springing up.

"It may be safely said that there is enough bluestone in Ulster County alone to keep the quarry portion of its population living for centuries to come," Charles E. Foote writing in Clearwater's History of Ulster County stated.

Today not a quarry is worked. The trails are overgrown. At Wilbur on the Kingston waterfront, a grotesque shambles of what was a handsome Victorian building is the last evidence that this was the center of the world of bluestone. This building contained offices of Simeon and William Fitch, whose firm started in 1839 and employed over 1500 men and more than 100 teams of horses by 1819. Elsewhere ghost villages mark other centers of this fabulous era. The industry is dead.

What is bluestone? What sustained the industry? And what

became of it? Technically, bluestone is a hard, close grained sandstone found in what geologists call the Hamilton Strata, a formation deposited millions of years ago during the Devonian Period. This description might satisfy a geologist whose chief interest is in classification, but the old quarryman who did not know when it was formed or what layer of earth contained it, knew many other things about it. He knew that to get it he had to "strip" tons of earth and stones before he reached a bluestone bed. He knew that a bluestone block was divided by natural vertical joints running north and south called "'side seams" and he knew that there were east to west joints called "headers" or "head offs". And he also knew that in addition to these vertical joints occurring anywhere from 5 to 75 feet apart, there were horizontal seams or reeds every 1 to 8 inches. He knew how to delicately tap wedges into the horizontal seams so that he could pry up perfect slabs of bluestone called 'lifts". Yes, and the quarryman knew many other things about his bluestone: how to split large lifts with precision by drilling a number of holes in a row and driving feathers and plugs into them with equal pressure until the strain caused the "lift" to come apart along the desired line. Later, a man named Knox showed him how to do it with a series of simultaneous tiny blasts. And he knew further, of other peculiarities like the fact that bluestone "worked" better north and south in Ulster County and east and west in Broome and Delaware counties. As an artist knows his brushes and paints, he knew the use of his tools: hammers, points, drills, wedges, crowbars, plugs and feathers, shovels, and even derricks. Yes - - all these things he knew about this blue treasure; but like all the other treasures in the Shawangunk and Catskill area there was one secret that kept its seekers from wealth. However, let us hold this detail until later in our story.

The bluestone industry had a brief and brilliant life. Although there are traditions of bluestone quarrying on Moray Hill in 1826, in Coeymans, near Albany in 1830, and other stories maintain that the first quarry was located in Sawkill about that time, there is definite evidence that the industry got its real start in 1832 when Silas Brainard began quarrying about 3 miles from Saugerties. He was a bridge builder from Connecticut who was working in Saugerties. He is reported to have visited the quarry at Coeymans and upon his return he noticed the same stone formations on the Van Wagenen farm near Saugerties. He bought this farm, began quarrying it and the bluestone era began.

At first the quarryman removed the stone from the earth, worked it into its final shape, transported it to the final market, and sold it. As time went on, it became an industry of specialists. The quarryman owned no land, but paid "'quarry rent", generally 5% of his selling price, to the land owner. The bluestone was transported from the quarries to the dealers by teamsters. The dealers located at the transportation center such as docks or railroad stations, bought from many quarries and fashioned the stone to the shapes required. Generally the dealer sold the stone to the builders in the cities but in some cases, a further step of organization saw a number of dealers combine to sell through one sales outlet.

The quarryman was a small independent businessman who employed a few people or perhaps just he and his partner did the work. He was the gambler to whom we shall return later. "Stone" a publication of the day had this to say about the quarryman. "The quarrying of bluestone probably requires as much skill, if not more, than any other kind of stone, a fact often overlooked and a potent factor in the success of a quarryman. It seems to be a general impression among a great many users and perhaps a few of the producers of this most useful and durable stone that a man needs only to find a deposit of salable quality, with the usual shipping facilities, and success is assured - - - - . As a rule, the best quarrymen have worked in the quarries from the time they have been able to do anything, and, as that is usually pretty early in life, many of them have gained such knowledge of the work that they know to a certainty how the stone will work, as soon as they see the bed, without raising a lift. It is only after long work that a quarryman becomes "expert' ". As we shall see this old quotation gave the quarryman credit for more than he knew, but it does give an idea of the type of man who "mined" for this blue gold. It was he who who had to rent the land, pay many months of wages to his employees and sustain his own family while a likely looking bluestone bed was "stripped" of the tremendous overlay of soil, clay and stone. It was he who often went into debt, and if his quarry was successful, it was he who hired more men and started stripping for more quarries. He was the real entrepreneur of the industry.

But there was a small class of man who reaped the rewards of the 49'er or of the oil fields of Texas. More often than not, his fabulous wealth was a result of pure luck and other people's labor. He was the landowner. In many cases he acquired land at one dollar an acre. This land had once been covered by dense Hemlock forests. Then in a furious period as brief, hectic, and prosperous as the bluestone era, the Tanneries of the Catskills denuded the slopes and destroyed the forests in a frantic grab for Hemlock bark, the life blood of the Tanneries. The trees gone, the Tanneries left, and this wasteland was sold at one dollar an acre. When bluestone was discovered on these lands, astronomical profits were made. Judge Hasbrouck had land that paid him $1500 per acre, land that paid him 1500% profit. Here indeed was Catskill treasure.

The other gambler in the bluestone picture was the teamster. He gambled with his life each day that he worked. He and his teams pulled "stone boats" down the sides of the mountains. These mountain boats were sledges made of four inch plank, fastened together to form platforms four feet by seven feet. These sledges wore deep gashes into the mountain sides. Loaded with tons of bluestone they tore out all underbrush, loose stones, and formed steep sided chutes down to the precipitous mountain roads where the stone was transferred to wagons. Each ride on these wagons was an adventure. In addition to four brake shoes, the rear wheels of the wagons were chained. Occasionally a chain would break or the brake shoes wouldn't hold and a tremendous bluestone juggernaut hurtled down the mountain. Many were the teamsters who lost their lives in that last frantic plunge.

The bluestone dealers were the great capitalists of the day. In their busy yards and mills the stones were divided into the three commercial categories: Flagstone: "edge" stone, and "rock".

Flagstone was stone about 1 1/2 inches thick with all edges at right angles to each other. It was used widely for sidewalks because it resisted wear due to its hardness. This same hardness, a result of its tight grain structure, also prevented it from absorbing moisture and therefore, its surface was never slippery. Flagstone unlike the other two classes, was usually worked at the quarry.

"Edge" stone was used for curbs, windows and door sills and other house trimmings. It required dressing on one or more surfaces and was worked into long rectangular blocks.

"Rock" was the name given to the rough large stones. The mills sawed them into various shapes such as steps, platforms, and building stone. The dealers also employed skilled stonecutters who created special products like mantles and ornamental designs for building facades.

It was the dealer who through his salesmen negotiated with the cities to flag their sidewalks with bluestone and with builders to decorate their buildings with it. The bluestone era from 1832 to about 1905 was the time of the great waves of immigration, the time of a great building boom and the old streets, office buildings, and mansions are the slowly disappearing testimony of bluestone's part in that expanding world.

It is a tragic thing to see a man cut down at the height of his power. So it was with the bluestone industry and this is why H. A. Haring in "Our Catskill Mountains" called his chapter on the industry, "The Tragedy of Bluestone". Two causes conspired to cause this sudden death.

First was the very perversity of quarrying. No amount of experience or examination nor even the proximity to a good quarry could insure a good bed of stone after the work and expense of stripping. The stone would look perfect. With trembling desperation the first wedges would be tapped into the lift seam. The most skilled hands would coax the tools into the stone. Suddenly the stone chips! Instead of lifting along a horizontal cleavage plane, a piece just breaks off. The process is repeated. Occasionally after several tries, lifts were obtained. However, more often than not the quarry was a dismal failure - - the months and money wasted.

Yet there were those moments of elation in which the wild shouts of the crew heralded the first successful lift. Then the lucky quarryman would push his luck by branching out. He might meet with several more successes and grow more rash. Ultimately and almost inevitably, a long slide of "tailings" down the side of the mountain would show the broken stones that were obtained in place of the flat and valuable slabs.

As the quarryman was forced further back into the mountains in his quest for good quarries, the expense of transportation mounted. His gamble became more desperate because his hope for profit decreased.

Then came the final blow - - Portland Cement. The age of concrete and cement began. Although hydraulic cement, cement which hardened after the addition of water, was not new, the improvements in Portland cement made for its rapid ascendancy. Indeed, the cement mines in the Rosendale area of Ulster County were world famous during the bluestone boom. It was a common sight on the bluestone docks at Wilbur to see canal boats passing by loaded with cement which had just reached tidewater after leaving the old Delaware and Hudson Canal through the Eddyville locks. This passing was symbolic. The convenience, the lower cost, and in many cases, the superiority of Portland cement were the final, crushing conditions which brought the end to the blue gold era of the Catskills.

The treasures that the Shawangunk and the Catskills reveal are transitory. The enduring treasures, precious metals and gems, have not been uncovered. The worldly hopes the men of Ulster set their hearts upon, the world soon passed by. The day of canal, the bluestone and even the cement is done. The quarries are overgrown with moss and vines. The canal bed is a neglected ditch which now holds sturdy young trees, trees which have had a sheltered start in its wind protected bosom. And strangest of all, the cement mines are vast, dank underground mushroom farms, except for a few macabre instances where a farsighted but pessimistic businessman has converted them to atomic bomb vaults.

WILLIAM THE SILENT.

Resorts /19

The Old Catskill Mountain House

"There are other stores of immense treasures just on the point of being revealed to the eager whites by the rude forefathers of the forest, but some good Indian either got drunk too soon or sober too soon, and the secret died with the departure of the dusky natives. Possibly the treasure reported was a sort of prophesy of the wealth that the summer tourists are now bringing into this mountainous region, and leaving here and there with the hotels, the boarding houses, the guides, the liverymen, and others. This source of wealth was 'hid away' in the trout streams, the ice caves, the mountain gorges, and the wild depths of the primeval forest, or perhaps the prophesy may be fulfilled in the quarries of bluestone now yielding their inexhaustible resources at the demands of business."

In 1880, N. B. Sylvester wrote these words in his "History

of Ulster County". And we have seen how Bluestone, the blue gold of the Catskills, did not fulfill this prophesy. But what of the hordes of summer tourists and the wealth that they bring? Will they prove to be the only perennial source of wealth, the one constant treasure that the mountains provide? Or will the hikers of the unborn generations pause to wonder at the tremendous overgrown ruins that mark the site of the teeming resort hotel of our day, as we now pause to marvel at the enterprise of our predecessors while exploring the abandoned quarry, the crumbling tannery foundations, the gaping canal bed, or the eerie underground vaults of the deserted cement mines.

The forerunners of the luxurious resort hotels of the Catskills and Shawangunks had such names as the "Hogs Back", "The Stratton Place", "Terrys" and "Garrisons". These were the roadside taverns where the teamsters hauling hides and leather between the tanneries of the Catskills and the docks at Rondout could stop for food, lodging and perhaps a little grog before the fire.

The identity of that latter day pioneer, the first summer boarder is lost to us, but what a hardy soul he must have been. The year was 1853 or 1854, according to De Lisser, and our summer tourist from New York City, who arrived at Rondout by steamer the previous day, arose at 5 in the morning. He clambered aboard a lumbering stagecoach of ancient vintage and set out on the half day shaking up that was required for the journey to Pine Hill. Then, if the wagon did not break down, or the two teams of horses quit from strain of tugging that jouncing load uphill through the serpentine quagmire called a road, then sometime around mid-day, he would arrive at the house of Monsieur Guigou, the first man to take summer boarders in the Catskills. Monsieur Guigou, a cultivated French gentleman, an exofficer in the army of Napoleon was a tanner of excellent repute. He must have been an excellent host too, because word spread and more boarders came. Of course, the real appeal was the rugged grandeur of the "mountains of the sky".

Still the summer boarder business was unimportant until the coming of the Ulster and Delaware Railroad in 1870. Then things began to boom. Great hotels and boarding houses sprang up. The area was highly advertised and the Railroad produced an annual book which listed the hotels and villages and described the mountains with such flowery prose as this, "Ever eloquent in their Creator's praise, they reach out a beckoning hand to enervated men and women the world over, to the discouraged and faltering worker, unfortunate idler and successful man of business", or "A breath of nature uncontaminated by the dregs of city civilization...."

While the railroad made the Catskills' unparalleled splendor accessible to the hordes of city dwellers, it also led to the growth of many of the large estates and game preserves deeper in the mountains where many rich families built summer homes. The Catskills experienced a great era in building in those few decades around the turn of the century.

In the nearby Shawangunks in 1869, two brothers, the twins, Alfred ii. and Albert K. Smiley, Quakers from Rhode Island discovered Skytop, Lake Mohonk and Minnewaska. From their profound impression of the jagged and spectacular area, sprang the world famous hotels at the two lake sites. The architecture and the landscaping preserved the rugged integrity of the area. The mountain top resorts were the scenes of many international conventions and the guestbook of its golden era reads like a diplomatic "Who's Who". Presidents and poets are among the guests. It was the site of an annual convention on Indian affairs and frequent councils on International arbitration.

In nearby Napanoch a wealthy advertising executive Mr. Frank Seaman opened the most exclusive hotel of the area. To Yama Farms, tastefully done in Japanese style, by invitations only, came such great men as the four cronies, Henry Ford, Thomas Edison, Harvey Firestone and John Burroughs, the great naturalist who knew and loved the Catskills and their wildlife as no man before or since.

Away from the Onteora Valley, in the southwestern part of the Catskills, chiefly in Sullivan County, an entirely different wave of building was going on. Here the teeming masses of recently arrived Jewish immigrants impelled a rapid evolution of the land, from farm, to boarding house, to hotel. Ulster had Jewish citizens in pre-revolutionary days, and in the early 1800's, when Utopian settlements sprang through the land, Sholam, a short lived Jewish cooperative settlement was created near the site of the Merriman Dam. However this new influx was due to the immigration from eastern Europe in the 1880's and 1890's. The first settlers of the new wave were interested in farming. They were men who were land hungry and some in ignorance bought farms that could not sustain their families. This created a need for a supplementary income that boarders might bring. During the vacation time, their spare rooms were eagerly taken by the immigrants who had settled in the lower east side of New York and who worked in the notorious needle trade sweat shops of the era. This latter group asked no more than to breathe fresh air and to relax during their brief vacations. The presence of their countrymen with facilities in the Catskills provided the ideal place. It was near enough to the city and they could avoid the embarrassment of language difficulties, dietary observations, and the strange customs that always frightened the newly arrived immigrant.

With this eager new market ready for them, the more enterprising farmers built boarding houses and in turn, the boarding houses became hotels. As in any business, under the duress of competition the more imaginative developed more attractive facilities and innovated recreational programs. Pressing beyond this, entertainment was introduced, first by the "social director" and then by travelling acts until the "Borscht Circuit" became one of the most famous training grounds for the American entertainment world. Many of the most famous stars of radio, films and television, served their apprenticeship in the hotels in the Catskills and the process is still going on.

In the early days of this great immigration, the older hotels of the area, forgetting that the original settlers in the 1600's spoke no English either, restricted their clientele. This practice which has since disappeared, served to isolate the two communities - - the old from the new. However, as naturalization progressed and a new native-born generation arose, old sentiments have virtually disappeared and the new generations are growing together with ever-increasing social harmony.

But what of the future of this resort industry, the last remaining treasure of the Catskills? Is the future secure? Several factors are at work and the result can only be prophesied. While the era of the hotel building was going on in the Catskill area, the nation and indeed the world, was experiencing two major revolutions which have profound bearing on the matter. The revolutions referred to are the dawn of the ages of low-priced rapid mass transportation and the age of mass communication.

At the turn of the century the automobile was a rarity, movies a crude process, and radio was still an idea. The multitudes of New York City with brief vacations had no private means to go where they chose. They went where public transportation could take them and they could not go too far because time was short. The influence of naturalists as Thoreau and Burroughs was strong and the people asked no more than to be in the country. Magazines and radios and movies of the day did not influence their recreation as they do today. It was not necessary to be fashionable, nor to emulate the heroes and heroines of Hollywood. The Catskills were eminently entertaining and so success was assured.

As time passed, it became progressively easier to travel longer distances, faster, and at lower prices. Any family that wasn't destitute and many that were, acquired an automobile which found an ever widening range as new roads were developed. While this was going on, the newspapers, magazines, radio and television assured the people that "communing with nature" was passe. It became necessary to learn the latest dance steps, to be seen in swankier hotels in other areas, and so the type of vacation one took, became a symbol of prestige, more and more, it has become unusual to spend more than one vacation in the same place. Somehow too, the idea has arisen that the farther away from home one gets, the better time one will have. Hence the growing popularity of air travel, cruises and package vacations.

All this has affected the Catskill resort area obviously. In Northern Ulster, the great hotels, old frame buildings of another period, are not being replaced. The rundown facilities are losing their ability to attract and accommodate present day tourists.

Many of the hotels of Southern Ulster and Sullivan Counties are still growing. These hotels keep abreast of the times, provide entertainment, golf, riding, swimming, tennis, dancing and all other recreations that today's generation demands. These tremendous vacation "factories" are huge enterprises employing hundreds of people and represent immense investments. They advertise widely and their success depends not on their location in the Catskills but upon the diverse facilities they have available. People no longer come merely to the mountains as they did in times gone by to enjoy the scenery. Is it likely that in time, the resort business will be concentrated in these huge enterprises? However, many families still continue to prefer the privacy of the bungalow colony and this branch of the resort industry is still growing vigorously.

There is another factor which should be mentioned. The last 10 years has seen the emergence of winter sports as a national pastime and with it, the winter vacation. Many ski-slopes have been installed in the mountains and the great New York State development at Belie Ayre Mountain has made the area, a skier's Mecca. Phoenicia, Pine Hill and Shandaken are bustling villages on winter weekends as colorfully dressed crowds of skiers mill along the streets. Keeping up with this development, bigger hotels have installed their own ski slopes.

How can this development be evaluated in terms of the long history of the area? Does it mark the emergence of an important new industry or will nature continue to thwart the seekers of wealth in the Catskills by continuing the climatic cycle in the direction of warmer winters with less snow. The evidence points in this direction.

Epilogue

As this book goes to press in May 1955 an unfinished tale of treasure must be included. If this treasure is found it will mean wealth for the Catskill area beyond the wildest dreams of all previous treasure hunters mentioned in this book. At this writing the treasure seems to lie in sight; but just beyond grasp. Another few weeks should tell whether the farmer who said, "No use sapping this spring, we're going to be rich soon," will be streaking through the Onteora Valley in a Cadillac or back boring holes in maple trees next spring.

In 1932 Ralph Longyear of Phoenicia called George Botchford to a well near Panther Mountain and showed him gas bubbles rising through the water. Tests proved that it was natural gas and they started the long process to exploit the wealth that they believed lay buried for eons beneath the constantly disappointing earth of the Catskills. Together with Clem and Henry Botchford the men began accumulating land leases and after ten year's they had acquired over 10,000 acres by promising to the owners one-eighth of all income produced by the leased land. By 1935 even the skeptical Dr. George Chadwick, New York State's senior geologist, was convinced that natural gas or oil could be found in a certain dome-like structure which he described. After one of his many field trips he assured George Botchford that he would be sorry if he ever gave it up.

The great depression years of the 1930's when no money was available were superseded by the great war years of the 1940's when neither men nor equipment could be had. As the 1950's rolled around the Botchford brothers and Ralph Longyear, now elderly men, realized that new blood and new money would be required to finance the tremendously expensive test drilling and exploration.

In 1953 these pioneers of Panther Mountain assigned their leases to the newly formed Dome Gas & Oil Corporation. This company is in turn a wholly owned subsidiary of North Star Oil & Uranium. In addition, a Mid-Hudson Natural Gas Corporation was formed to conduct explorations in adjacent areas. Dome Gas & Oil Corporation is drilling the first test well on the Herdman Farm just outside of Shandaken, a village whose early tanbark wealth is again reappearing, thanks to trout, deer, and ski-slopes.

The present officers of Dome Gas & Oil Corporation are Stuart Curry of Hamilton, New York, president; Martin Rubin and Dick Atwater, vice-presidents. Mr. Rubin is a well known Phoenicia attorney while for Atwater, who was born in Australia and who is field superintendent, has wild-catted in Oklahoma, South Dakota, Pennsylvania, and Wyoming.

Another word from the tangled world of corporate finance

should be entered. Dome Gas & Oil has an exclusive arrangement with Transcontinental Gas & Oil which operates gas lines between Texas and New York City, to supply all the gas that Dome can produce to the towns of Shandaken, Lexington, Hardenburgh, Middletown, Woodstock,, Denning, Hunter, Olive, and Halcott. It should also be mentioned that New York State Natural Gas Company, a subsidiary of Standard Oil of New York, has begun buying leases in the area paying one dollar per acre per year.

While over 500,000 shares of stock, some of it in the hands of some 400 Catskill Mountain people, has been changing hands and rising from fifty cents per share to one dollar per share, Dick Atwater and his crew of drillers have been busy. Drilling began in April 1954 and gas showed from the start. At times the gas escaping from the well casing was ignited and citizens and neighbors flocked like moths to the golden glare of the yard-high jet flame, their bright eyes reflecting bright prospects. By the time the traditionally productive Oriskany Sands were hit at about 5,300 feet the well was producing about 50,000 cubic feet of gas per day; but at least 250,000 cubic feet is required for a good commercial well. After consulting with Transcontinental Gas & Oil, Dome continued down to the Clinton Sands at 6,400 feet. Here drilling stopped. The very generous Botchford brothers, the informative Mr. Martin Rubin, and the "old pro" Dick Atwater have very kindly brought the author up to date in a series of calls and visits.

For a final summary of the way the waiting wealth reposes we reprint in its entirety the following story from the May 13, 1955 issue of the Catskill Mountain News with the kind permission of its editor, Mr. Clark Sandford.

NUCLEAR TEST MADE OF DOME GAS WELL TO LEARN NEW DATA

Gamma and Neutron Rays Record Formations
Of Rock 6,400 Feet Below Shandaken Farm;
Will Show If Gas Flow Can Be Increased

Faith in the existence of natural gas in commercial quantities may be justified if the results of the most complete scientific analysis yet made of the Dome Gas and Oil well in Shandaken are favorable. A nuclear test of the well, which is down to 6,400 feet, was made Friday, May 13th, 1955, to determine how much gas is under the Amasa Herdman farm, and where it is, if there is commercial gas there.

The test was sponsored by the Transcontinental Pipeline Corp., which has had an interest in the well since last fall, when it contracted with the Dome Gas & Oil Corp. to buy all the gas the well produces. The first favorable showing of natural gas was reached in January about the 5,300-foot level. Since then small pockets have been struck, but the elusive rock dome, where the gas is believed to be abundant, has remained out of reach of the huge drill bit.

The test was conducted by the Schlumberger Well Service, an international organization which specializes in making analyses of all types of wells. Film-recorded "readings" made by gamma and neutron rays from within the well casing will be analyzed this week. These will help decide future steps in the development of Catskill's first gas well.

From these readings will be determined the nature and location of each of the "sand" or rock structures through which the well has been pierced. The gamma rays will determine how porous the structures are and how permeable or to what degree they can be filled with gas. These rays also measure any quantities of gas found.

The neutron rays record any show of gas, measure and locate the gas, if any shows. Both rays can be operated inside or without the well casing. In the case of the Herdman well, they were operated from inside the six-inch casing.

The rays send their impulses through a long cable from which the apparatus is suspended. In a specially equipped truck, they are transmitted to a long roll of film in the form of zig-zag lines. The greater the waver of the line, the more porous is the rock structure being tested.

The neutron gun used in the test is owned by the Canadian Government and loaned to the Schlumberger company. Before it could be used at Shandaken, it had to be insured for $20,000 to cover loss in case it was destroyed during the test.

Richard Atwater Jr., superintendent in charge at the Dome Gas and Oil well, said that he would be able to "fish" the apparatus from the well casing in the event a cable broke. With a twinkle, Mr. Atwater added that in case that was unsuccessful, for $20,000 he would go into the casing, himself, to retrieve the apparatus. However, the operation was carried out without a mishap.

The neutron gun was encased in a heavy lead shield on a small wheeled cart, While the technicians were removing it from the case, no one was allowed on the rig floor because of the danger from radiation. The technicians said that the apparatus, when out of its shield, could cause serious illness and death to anyone absorbing the radiation.

Since the discovery of the initial large pocket of gas at the well in late January, drilling has been continued to search for the main deposit. Frequent pockets of gas have been struck, lending encouragement as the well probed deeper. If the results of Friday's tests are satisfactory, Dome will know where to hydrofract, a process by which rock formations are broken down by the water to release gas. It is expected that a considerable amount of knowledge will be gained, pointing the way to a second well.

Mr. Atwater hopes to have the results of the findings in a week or ten days. When obtained they will be made public. In Pennsylvania gas fields where hydro-fracturing has been tried by several companies, the flow of gas from the wells has been multiplied several times. The approximate open flow of the Herdman well is 50,000 cubic feet daily. Fracturing of Pennsylvania wells of the same flow has increased the flow from zero at one well to 142 times at another well. The average increase after fracturing is 16.

Recently chip samples of the last 20 feet of the Clinton sands, where the bottom of the Herdman well now is, were taken. These also are being analyzed for porosity and other factors.

The North Star Oil and Uranium Corp. has received 200,000 shares of common stock of the Mid-Hudson Natural Gas Corp., in return for an agreement for interchange of geological data in the area. The Mid-Hudson Corporation has 6,000 acres under lease in Ulster, Delaware and Greene counties, adjoining the areas in which Dome Gas and Oil Corp. is operating. Mid-Hudson is negotiating leases on more than 10,000 additional acres.

North Star will distribute 12,500 shares of the Mid- Hudson stock to North Star stockholders at the rate of one share of Mid-Hudson for each 20 shares of North Star held.

As Time Goes By

It is hard to believe that 43 years have passed since the completion of the previous sentence and the one I am presently writing. The last chapter of *Treasure Tales of the Shawangunks and Catskills* dealt with the exploration and expectation of finding natural gas in the local mountains. The book went to press before the results of these programs could be determined. History could have predicted it for us.

Like its predecessors, this vaporous treasure was present but not in commercial quantities. Nevertheless, there have been other natural gifts from our mountains. The bountiful springtime run-off from the mountain snows is channeled, guided and collected through an intricate network of waterways to replenish the reservoirs.

The bluestone, the cement, the tanneries, and the ice harvesting industries which employed thousands of local workers have been made obsolete by technological developments. The cycle of large ornate, burgeoning and then decaying north Catskill resorts has repeated itself. The latter day southern Catskill hotels are facing the impending oblivion of their predecessors. Perhaps the intervention of large well capitalized companies, which participate in many phases of the leisure time industries, will find it worthwhile to invest in this area.

On a more optimistic note, the local historical organizations that are active today such as: The D&H Canal Historical Society, The Woodstock Historical Association, The Catskill Art Society and Museum, and other similar groups are enjoying excellent support as well as enthusiastic participation by their members, many of whom have become residents of our area. Perhaps we are all seeking roots and attachments to certain unique places that will allow us to enjoy that profound relationship with a parcel of land we can call our own. As Brigham Young said, "This is the place."

Alf Evers

Baseball historians recall for us that its most famous double play combination was "Tinker to Evers to Chance." Our Alf Evers has left nothing to chance. The thoroughness of his research, the lucidity of his writing, and the magnitude of his output make him the dean of local historians, and indeed his reputation enjoys much broader horizons. His magnum opus, *The Catskills From The Wilderness To Woodstock*, has become the authoritative reference text for scholars interested in this region.

When I called Alf to ask him to write the preface for this second edition, he told me that his eyesight was failing and that he had to give up the use of his word processor. He kindly offered to write it by hand, but he doubted that I would be able to read his scrawl. I assured Alf that I would find someone who could decipher it. I did with the help of some friendly cryptographers. Afterwards, we had a chance to chat for a while, In the course of the conversation, Alf mentioned that he was 93 years old. My rejoinder informed him that I was 75; whereupon he commented that I was still a youngster, but that I showed great promise.

Despite the fact that his written output is so broad, I was amazed by his ability to remember details of events that occurred many decades ago. This ability enables him to place local events into broad historical context. His familiarity with the field is awesome.

The Japanese have a tradition of recognizing and rewarding their most gifted elderly masters. Artists, potters, poets and other outstanding creative individuals are formally designated as National Treasures. Surely, Alf Evers is one of our National Treasures, one of the few I have encountered on my journey. He is indeed a rare talent from whom we will continue to learn and to enjoy in the years to come.

The Ice Age

The decades of the 1920s and 30s were an era of unprecedented transformation in almost every facet of American life, as technology bestowed its not always favorable bounty upon us. Not only products but also complete industries were made obsolete. The buggy whip, the magic lantern, and more significantly, the Hudson River's ice harvesting industry melted away like a cake of ice on a hot tin roof.

The rise and fall of the ice industry was but a blink of an eye of history. Its decline was foretold by the introduction, construction and expansion of the nation' s electric power grid, which in turn gave rise to the avalanche of domestic electrical appliances, including radio and television. The growing popularity of the automobile and the introduction to the age of flight led to the establishment of support systems including the petroleum, rubber, and allied service industries, along with the ever-expanding highway system. While all aspects of American life felt the overwhelming demands for change that the new industries imposed upon the patterns of our basically rural society, there were many improvements and conveniences. These new products and processes relieved the debilitating and often degrading labor demands both at home and in the work place.

One of the least chronicled developments brought about by this time of transition was the demise of the Hudson River ice industry. During its heyday, this industry employed thousands of men who cut the ice and transported it to huge multi-storied, insulated warehouses along the River. Each year as warm weather approached, they gradually withdrew the frozen inventory of blocks of ice. Then they loaded them onto specially designed barges that transported them to New York City. These barges were instantly recognizable because of the large windmill that sat atop a small cabin on the stern of each barge. The windmills powered the pumps that drained the melt water from the hold. The melt water would constantly accumulate and would be potentially dangerous if large volumes of uncontrolled water surged back and forth with the rocking of the craft threatening the stability of the barge. After docking, the barges were unloaded onto the horse drawn wagons that waited alongside the dock. From there they were dispatched to the homes that had placed orders for them. Actually, it was a piece of the River itself which was the commodity that was finally delivered to the customer.

Although there is no question that refrigeration and air conditioning improved the quality of life, there are few other instances where the introduction of a new technology so rapidly and irrevocably eliminated a thriving industrial activity.

I still remember the rite of passage that conferred upon me the privilege and responsibility of emptying the flat, disk-shaped basin to be found under every icebox. Neophytes often spilled water on the floor because they did not observe the conservative one-inch distance from the surface of the water to the rim of the basin, nor were they strong enough to hold the heavy weight steady while carrying it. The need of the icebox for timely attention was almost organic.

In summer, children waited for the ice wagon to arrive so they could plead for a chewable chunk of ice to experience that rare frozen treat, despite the fact that it had no flavor. Their entreaties were usually recognized by the iceman, an awesome individual who deftly set his tongs in a single sweep, clamped them onto the ice block, and easily lifted it over his shoulder. He was the role model that came to mind when we thought about strong men. His very presence was intimidating enough to keep us from even considering helping ourselves to a piece of the ice.

The multitudes of workers and animals out on the ice during the winter months created a need for a group that specialized in removing the tinted effluent of man and beast. They were called "shine boys" and their numbers rose and fell reflecting the rise and demise of the Hudson River's ice harvesting industry. Now there was a new way to organize the indispensable transition from water to ice and back again to water.

Alf Evers recalls that as a boy he lived not far from the Hudson's west bank and now has many personal recollections of the waning days. One example was the fairly frequent occasions when a huge blaze lit up the sky with a bright orange glow. Everyone would understand its meaning: "There goes another ice house."

Now for a prideful personal note. My daughter Wendy has been employed for the past ten years as a senior archaeologist in a federal agency. She is a past-President of the Professional Archaeologists of New York City (PANYC). In 1998, she was elected to the Board of the New York Archaeological Council. She has written many professional papers, some of which concern subjects touched upon in this book, particularly the ice harvesting industry of the Hudson Valley. The following is an abstract of a paper she and her long-time associate Arnold Pickman presented at the 1998 Conference of the Society for Historical Archaeology in Atlanta, Georgia:

"Harris, Wendy Elizabeth and Pickman, Arnold. Frozen in Time: Hudson River Landscape Transformations and the Ice Industry. This paper examines riverine landscape transformations in the Hudson River Valley and their economic, technological, social and cultural correlates. The focus is on the transformation of the visual landscape resulting from the development of the natural ice industry in the second half of the nineteenth century. Past and contemporary representations of this landscape have emphasized its pastoral qualities and minimized the extent to which the waterway was engineered and industrialized in the nineteenth and early twentieth centuries. Consequently the history of the ice industry, and the built environment associated with it, has been obscured. Subsequent changes to shoreline terrain and ecology have eradicated all but archaeological evidence of this once vibrant rural industry.

Today, dominant 'natural' elements are celebrated thus robbing the landscape of its history. Plans for future land use are influenced by such contradictions."

It was her interest in this subject that aroused my curiosity about the ice industry. There is not much information available from a single source, so it's quite a luxury to have a resident scholar with sources that include obscure publications in the files of regional historical associations and museums.

There is a legend older than any related here and indeed, older than Ulster. It might have been written about works and aspirations of the Shawangunks and the Catskills. It tells of a king who wanted an inscription that would be true for 1,000 years, and even beyond that, to the end of the world. An inscription which could not be refuted, changed, or ridiculed, and he ordered his wise men to write it.

They wrote,
"*And this too shall pass away.*"

Should auld ac·quaintance be for·got and nev·er brought to mind?

Bibliography

Beers, F. W., *County Atlas of Ulster, New York*. New York
    Walker and Jewett, 36 Vesey Street. 1875
Brink, Benjamin Meyer, *The Early History of Saugerties*
    1660. Kingston, N. Y. R. C.rr. Anderson and Son. 1902
Brodhead, John Romeyn, *History of the State of New York*
    (2 Vols.) New York. Harper and Bros. 1871
Carmer, Carl, *The Hudson*. New York. Rinehart and Co., Inc.
Clearwater, Alphonso T., *The History of Ulster County New York*.
    Kingston, N. Y. V.J. Van Deusen. 1907
De Lisser, R. Lionel, *Picturesque Ulster*. Kingston, N. Y.
    The Styles and Bruyn Publishing Co. 1896
De Vries, David Peterson, *Voyages from Holland to America*.
    New York. 1853
De Witt, VSrilliam C., *People's History of Kingston, Rondout,
    and Vicinity* 1820-1843. New Haven, Conn. 1943
Dickinson, Harold T., *Quarries of Bluestone and Sandstones*.
    University of the State of New New York State Museum.
    Albany. 1903
Eager, Samuel W., A, *Outline History of Orange County*.
    Newburgh. S. T. Callahan. 1846-7
Friel, Arthur O., *Cat O'Mountain*. New York. A. L. Burt Co. 1923

Friel, Arthur O., *Hard Wood*. Philadelphia. Penn Publishing Co.   1925
Goodwin, Maud Wilder, *Dutch and English on the Hudson*.
    New Haven. Yale University Press. 1920
Gray, Elizabeth H., *Old Nirtety-Niners' Cave*. Boston.
    The C.M. Clark Publishing Co. 1909
Gumaer, Peter E., *A History of Deerparle in Orange County, N. Y.*
    Minisink Valley Historical Society, 1890
Haring, H. A., *Our Catskill Mountains*. New York. G. P.
    Putnam's Sons. 1931
Hickey, Andrew S., *The Story of Kingston*.   New York   Stratford
House, 52 Vanderbilt Avenue   1952
Hine, C. G., *The Old Mine Road*. Hine's Annual. 1908
Ingersoll, Ernest, *Illustrated Guide to the Hudson River and Catskill*
    Mountains. Chicago and New York: Rand McNally & Co. 1893
Johnson, Clifton, *The Picturesque Hudson*. New York
    The Macmillan Company, 1909
Johnson, P. Demarest, Cladius, *The Cowboy of the Ramapo Valley*.
    Middletown, N.Y. Slausonand Boyd Press Steam Print. 1894
Le Roy, Edwin D., *The Delaware and Hudson Canal*.
    The Wayne County Historical Society, 1950
Longstrerh, T. Morris, *The Catskills*. New York. The Century Co., 1921
Rockwell, Rev. Charles, *The Catskill Mountains and the Region Around*.
    New York. Taintor Bros. and Co., 229 Broadway. 1861
Schoonmaker, Marius, *The History of Kingston*. New York
    Purr Printing House, 18 Jacob Street. 1888
Smith, Philip H., *Legends of the Shawangunk and Its Environs*.
    Pawling, N. Y. Smith and Co. 1887
Stickney, Charles E., *A History of the Minisink Region*.
    Middletown, N. Y. Coe Pinch and I. F. Guiwits. 1867
Sylvester, Nathaniel Bartlett, *History of Ulster County*,
    New York. Philadelphia. Everts and Peck. 1880
Van Buren, Augustus H., *A History of Ulster County Under the*
    Dominion of the Dutch. Kingston, N. Y.   1923
Wilstach, Paul, *Hudson River Landings*.   Indianapolis.
    The Bobbs-Merrill Company 1933

JOURNALS AND PERIODICALS

Olde Ulster - Benjamin M. Brink - Kingston, New York.
Proceedings of the Ulster County Historical Society
    Kingston, New York.
Proceedings of the New York State Historical Association
    Newburgh, New York.